'Why do you [...]
What are you [...]

'I've no idea wh[...] [...]
another step but he still didn't move aside.

'So it isn't a conscious reaction, then? You don't deliberately pull up the drawbridge every time you feel someone is getting too close for comfort?'

'I don't know what you're talking about, Matt. I was never any good at solving riddles.' She brushed past him and opened the front door. 'I'll see you in the morning. Goodnight.'

'Goodnight, Catherine.'

He didn't try to detain her any longer.

Catherine got into her car, trying to ignore the empty ache inside her, the feeling that she had turned her back on something very special. Matt was just a colleague and he would never be any more than that.

She knew it was true, yet no matter how hard she tried she couldn't convince herself she had done the right thing by walking away from him. Part of her wished she'd stayed.

Jennifer Taylor lives in the north-west of England with her husband Bill. She had been writing Mills & Boon® romances for some years, but when she discovered Medical Romances™, she was so captivated by the heart-warming stories that she set out to write them herself! When she is not writing or doing research for her latest book, Jennifer's hobbies include reading, travel, walking her dog and retail therapy (shopping!). Jennifer claims all that bending and stretching to reach the shelves is the best exercise possible.

Recent titles by the same author:

A VERY SPECIAL MARRIAGE
SAVING DR COOPER

THE DOCTOR'S CHRISTMAS GIFT

BY
JENNIFER TAYLOR

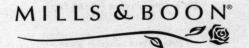

All the characters in this book have no existence outside the imagination of the author, and have no relation whatsoever to anyone bearing the same name or names. They are not even distantly inspired by any individual known or unknown to the author, and all the incidents are pure invention.

First published in Great Britain 2003
Harlequin Mills & Boon Limited,
Eton House, 18-24 Paradise Road, Richmond, Surrey TW9 1SR

© Jennifer Taylor 2003

ISBN 0 263 83482 4

Set in Times Roman 10½ on 11 pt.
03-1103-57746

Printed and bound in Spain
by Litografía Rosés, S.A., Barcelona

CHAPTER ONE

'DR FIELDING shouldn't be long now. He's running late tonight…again! I was just on my way home but if you'd like to wait in here then I'll tell him you've arrived.'

'Thank you.'

Catherine Lewis looked around the room as the receptionist hurried away. It was quite a pleasant room, she decided, taking stock. Brookdale Surgery was sited in one of the old Victorian terraces that overlooked the park and the room had a typically spacious feel with its high ceiling and generous proportions.

There were chairs lined up against the walls and a table in the centre stacked with magazines. A poinsettia in a glazed earthenware pot made a splash of colour against its polished surface. It looked exactly like the waiting room in a lot of GP's surgeries, in fact—a little untidy and slightly the worse for wear. When she opened her own surgery, she would make sure the waiting room looked much better than this.

Catherine walked to the window and looked out but there wasn't much to see. It was the middle of October and dark outside. Pushing back the cuff of her suit jacket, she checked the time. Six forty-two. Her interview had been scheduled for six-thirty and although she had no other engagements that evening it was annoying to be kept waiting. She was always punctual both in her professional and her private life. To her mind, it was not only bad manners to keep people waiting but a sign of inefficiency. Recalling what the receptionist had said, it appeared that punctuality wasn't one of Dr Fielding's strong points. It made her wonder how they would get on.

5

'Dr Lewis. I'm so sorry to have kept you waiting.'

Catherine swung round when she heard the man's voice. Her eyes were dazzled by the lights in the room so that she couldn't see him clearly. She had a fleeting impression of height and breadth of shoulder as he came towards her. He stopped and held out his hand, his face breaking into a warm smile which immediately made her want to smile back. She was so surprised that she found herself giving in to the impulse.

'I'm Matthew Fielding. We spoke on the phone the other day.'

His fingers felt warm and slightly rough against the smoothness of hers. Catherine let her hand remain in his for a moment longer than politeness dictated before she realised what she was doing. She quickly withdrew her hand, curbing the urge to run it down her skirt to remove the slight tingling sensation. She cleared her throat, not sure she enjoyed the fact that she could still feel the impression Matthew Fielding's fingers had left on hers.

'I'm delighted to meet you, Dr Fielding.' She smoothed her face into a suitable expression, pleased that she had managed to control the inane smile at last. She didn't *feel* nervous but maybe she was. After all, this job was another step in the right direction, another rung to be climbed on the ladder towards her goal.

The thought helped her focus on what was really important rather than the strange way she seemed to be behaving that night. She had made her plans a long time ago and not once had she veered from the route she had chosen—A levels, med school, experience in a variety of suitable general practices before she opened her own surgery. Now all she needed was a year here at Brookdale Surgery, a practice in an increasingly popular area of the city, then she would be ready to start looking for suitable premises…

'So I'd really love a cup of coffee—wouldn't you?'

Catherine jumped when she realised that she'd missed what Matthew Fielding had said. A little colour touched her cheeks at the lapse. She prided herself on always being focused and it wasn't like her to let her mind wander.

'I...um...coffee would be nice,' she said, hoping that she had guessed correctly what he'd been saying. It seemed that she had because he smiled at her once more. He really did have the most wonderful smile, she thought. It was so warm and friendly that it must make people *long* to confide in him.

Catherine took a quick breath when she realised her thoughts were wandering again. It was a relief when Matthew turned to lead the way out of the room. She kept her eyes locked on his back as she followed him into the corridor, hoping it would help if she concentrated on something tangible. She *must* be nervous. It was the only explanation that made any sense.

He had to be well over six feet tall, she decided, her gaze sweeping up the solid length of his muscular back. He moved with the easy grace of a trained athlete, his long legs striding purposefully along the corridor so that she had to quicken her pace to keep up. Her brown eyes skimmed over the neat hips and trim waist, the wide shoulders, before moving up to his well-shaped head.

His hair was a rich, sandyblond colour, very thick and crisp-looking. He wore it cut very short, probably because it had a tendency to curl if he allowed it to grow any longer. Catherine sighed wistfully as she thought how typical it was that a man should be blessed with that kind of hair. Her own hair was so straight that she'd long since given up any hope of making it curl. Now she rarely bothered to do anything different with it, preferring to wear it the way she wore it that night—neatly coiled into a heavy, nut-brown knot at the nape of her neck.

Someone—a man who had hoped to become rather more than a friend—had told her once that she should let her hair down both physically and metaphorically speaking. However, it was a piece of advice she had never heeded.

She preferred to keep all aspects of her life strictly under control.

'I hope you don't mind if we use the kitchen.' Matthew Fielding paused and looked back at her, a hint of amusement making his blue eyes sparkle. 'I know it isn't usual to conduct an interview around the kitchen table but I haven't eaten all day. I'm sure you would prefer not to have to give a practical demonstration of your skills, Catherine, if I passed out from lack of sustenance!'

Catherine felt a frisson run under her skin when he addressed her by her first name. It was odd how disturbing it was to have him call her that, as though they had crossed some unseen boundary. She gave a small shrug, not wanting him to guess there was anything wrong.

'Wherever is most convenient for you, Dr Fielding. I really don't mind.'

'Make that Matthew. Or better still, Matt. That's what most people call me, or at least those I class as friends.' He opened the door then stepped back to let her precede him.

Catherine smiled politely as she went into the room although she took care neither to agree nor disagree with his suggestion. She had no qualms about calling him Matthew once their relationship was established, but as for using the diminutive…

She shivered, wondering why the thought of being classed as one of his friends bothered her so much. She had a wide circle of friends, all of them people like her who understood exactly what constituted *friendship*. They followed the rules and accepted there were limits to what a friend could be called upon to do. There should be no exchanges of confidences, no unannounced visits, no demands other than the brief sharing of time at various social events. That Matthew Fielding would view friendship as something entirely different went without question although Catherine had no idea how she could possibly have known that.

It was yet another niggling little worry, another uncertainty, and her mouth pursed. How *did* she know that Matthew Fielding would expect a lot more from someone he classed as his friend?

'Sugar? Milk?' Matthew had plugged in the kettle and was now taking mugs out of a cupboard. Catherine forced her mind back on track again. Maybe this was a rather strange place to hold an interview but she mustn't allow it to upset her.

'Just milk please,' she replied evenly, pulling out a chair and sitting down at the big pine table. She glanced round the kitchen and realised immediately that it wasn't just somewhere the staff made themselves a drink during the day. It was a real family kitchen, from the bright yellow Aga to the childish drawings fixed to the refrigerator door by a selection of colourful magnets. She frowned uncertainly, wondering what the arrangements were within the practice.

'I live here in the main part of the house. There's just the kitchen on the ground floor, though, because the rest of the space is needed for the surgery,' Matthew informed her. He opened the fridge and took out a bottle of milk. He splashed some into a mug then brought it over to the table for her.

'Thank you.' Catherine smiled politely but she couldn't pretend that she wasn't surprised by what she'd learned. She hadn't realised that the surgery was essentially part of Matthew's home although she had no idea what difference it made.

'You're welcome.'

Once again she was treated to one of those wonderful smiles before he went back to the refrigerator and dug around inside it for a moment. He had a head of lettuce and a couple of tomatoes in his hands this time when he slammed the door.

'As I was saying, the main part of the house is also my home, which makes it very handy for getting to work of a morning. No such thing as traffic jams to contend with...well, not vehicular ones, anyway.'

He grinned as he plonked the lettuce on a chopping board and set to work. Catherine watched as he expertly shredded it then set about slicing the tomatoes. It was obvious that he was used to doing such tasks because his hands never faltered when he carried on speaking.

'When Glenda and I decided to open the practice we realised that one of us would have to live over the shop so to speak. It was a question of economics. Property in the city is horrendously expensive, as you know, so there was no way that we could afford to buy or even lease suitable premises.'

'I see. So you decided to combine the two and make your home here?'

'That's right. I was married by then and Ruth, my wife, was expecting our first child. The plan was that we would live here until the practice got on its feet and then we would move out of the city. However, after Ruth died it made more sense to continue living here. It means that I don't have to waste time travelling to and from work and can be home with the children as soon as I finish.' He put down his knife and went back to the fridge.

Catherine frowned as she tried to absorb what he had told her. She'd had no idea that Matthew Fielding was a widower although there was no reason why she should have known, of course. His domestic arrangements had little to do with her except where they overlapped into his work. She waited until he had found what he needed in the fridge, which turned out to be a bowl of large brown eggs this time, before she set about clarifying the situation.

'And Glenda—who I assume is your partner in the practice—is quite happy with the arrangement?'

'Oh, yes. And, yes, again, Glenda is indeed my partner. Sorry. I should have explained that at the beginning.' He grinned at her. 'Just because I know so much about you, it doesn't mean that you know anything about me, or this practice for that matter. Feel free to fire away and ask me anything you want.'

Catherine smiled coolly but it was just a cover for the fact that she couldn't think of a single question to ask him at that moment. Maybe it was because the interview wasn't following the usual pattern which had thrown her off course, she reasoned. Whenever she had been interviewed in the past there had been all the usual questions about her educational achievements, her experience and future plans, but Matthew Fielding hadn't touched on any of those points so far.

All of a sudden, she found herself willing him to get back on track. Silly though it sounded, but she knew it would be easier to cope if she was on familiar ground. However, it seemed that he had no intention of fitting in with her preconceived ideas about how to conduct an interview.

'Don't tell me you're too shy to ask me any questions, Catherine.' He looked expectantly at her and she was mortified to feel herself blushing.

Matthew shook his head, a rueful expression crossing his face. 'Me and my big mouth, eh? Of course you're shy. You only met me five minutes ago and you're probably on your best behaviour and don't want to appear pushy. It's a long time since I went for an interview so you'll have to forgive me.'

'I…um… There's nothing to forgive.'

The situation was rapidly deteriorating and Catherine knew that she had to do something before it got any worse. Matthew had made her sound like some delicate little soul who was afraid to say boo to the proverbial goose rather than a mature woman of thirty-two who was more than capable of running her own life! She sat up straighter, a touch of hauteur about the look she gave him.

'I assure you that I am not shy, Dr Fielding. However, you were right to say that I know very little about this practice apart from what you told me over the phone.'

She took a deep breath, pleased to hear how composed she sounded. It gave her the confidence to continue although she would have preferred it if Matthew had sat down rather than carried on with what he was doing. Her tone sharpened as she watched him breaking eggs into a bowl.

'So Glenda is Dr Williams, and there are just the two of you in practice here at Brookdale Surgery?'

'That's right.' He picked up a fork and began beating the eggs. 'We have been toying with the idea of finding a third partner as the practice is expanding so fast. You may have heard that this area is becoming one of the most sought-after in London.'

His tone was dry when he said that and Catherine frowned. It hadn't sounded as though the idea pleased him although surely it should? A thriving population would bring many rewards to the practice. With more patients on his list, Matthew could apply for extra funding. He could even take on private patients if he wanted to because there were always people willing to pay if it meant they could avoid the NHS queues. It was all very puzzling but she decided that it might be best not to question him. It really wasn't her business how he felt.

'So I believe. However, the job you advertised wasn't for a third partner,' she stated coolly.

'No. We've put that idea on hold for now. We have a far more pressing problem to deal with at the moment.'

He opened a cupboard and took out a heavy iron pan. Setting it on the Aga, he scooped a knob of butter from the dish and dropped it into the pan. As soon as it began to sizzle he added the egg mixture to the pan then turned to look at her.

'Glenda has just found out that she's pregnant. Naturally, she's thrilled because she and her husband have been trying for a baby for ages. However, she's had a couple of miscarriages in the past so her obstetrician has advised her that she should stop work immediately to give herself the best chance possible of carrying this baby to term.

'I've arranged locum cover to tide us over for a few weeks but Glenda and I both agreed that we need something more permanent. And that's where you come in, Catherine.'

Once again she felt that ripple under her skin when he called her by her first name. Catherine steadfastly ignored it, choosing instead to concentrate on the professional aspects of this strange interview, although it wasn't easy in the circumstances. Holding an interview in a kitchen really wasn't her idea of how things should be done.

Matthew had returned his attention to his cooking and was now lifting the omelette from the pan. He smiled at her, one sandy brow rising a fraction. 'If you want half, just say the word.'

She shook her head, wishing he would concentrate on what they were there for. Silly though it sounded, the sooner this was over the happier she would feel. There was something a little too *familiar* about the thought of them sitting around the kitchen table sharing a meal. It troubled her. 'Thank you but I've already eaten.'

It wasn't a lie because she'd had a cup of coffee and a sandwich on her way there that night. There hadn't been time for anything more substantial after she'd finished the early evening surgery which she had been rostered for that day. However, she couldn't stop her stomach from suddenly rumbling when her nostrils caught the tantalising aroma which wafted across the kitchen.

Matthew laughed as he took a second plate off the shelf and deftly slid half the omelette onto it. 'Stop being so polite! Here you go.'

Before Catherine could protest he had put the plate in front of her and gone to fetch another set of cutlery. He sat down, offering her the bowl of salad so that she had no option but to take some.

'Thank you,' she said stiffly, cutting a sliver off the omelette and popping it into her mouth. It tasted wonderful, she realised. Light and fluffy and a world better than her own miserable efforts.

'You're welcome.' Matthew tucked into his meal with unselfconscious relish. He forked a mouthful of salad into his mouth and quickly chewed it. 'Anyway, I've read your references and everything, and there's no problem there. You're more than qualified for this post from what I've seen so far.'

'But?' Catherine paused in the act of popping another sliver of omelette into her mouth when she caught the reservation in his voice.

'Not really a *but*.' He smiled reassuringly. 'I just find it odd that someone with your talent hasn't found a permanent position. You've worked in...what? Five different practices since you qualified?'

'Six, actually, if you count where I did my GP rotation.'

She pushed the plate away, wanting to concentrate on the reason why she was there rather than allowing herself to be sidetracked. 'I suppose it does seem strange from your point of view, but I assure you that the reason I haven't taken a permanent post isn't because of a lack of offers. On the contrary, every practice I have worked for so far has offered me a job, including my present employer.'

'But that isn't what you want? Why not?'

He tipped back in his chair and regarded her thoughtfully. Catherine realised with a little start of surprise that beneath the easygoing manner lay a very astute mind. Matthew Fielding wasn't a man who would allow anyone to pull the wool over his eyes, but as she had no intention of doing that, it wasn't a problem.

'Because I don't want to work for someone else. My intention has always been to set up my own practice.' She shrugged but her brown eyes were steady when they met his. 'That's why I only ever accept jobs which will further my experience and why I never stay in them longer than a year. Each post I've had has been simply a stepping-stone towards my ultimate goal.'

'And working here at Brookdale Surgery will be another of those stepping-stones? Is that what you are saying?'

He sounded amused by the idea and Catherine smiled although she didn't share his amusement. Didn't he realise how serious she was about this and how much time and effort she had put into bringing her plans to fruition?

'Yes. That's right. The experience I gain here will be invaluable when I open my own practice,' she explained calmly.

'And what if I offered you a permanent post once your contract is up? Is there anything that would make you change your mind—the offer of a partnership, for instance?'

She shook her head. 'No. I know exactly what I want, Dr Fielding, and there is no way that I would give up everything I've worked so hard to achieve.'

'Then you are a very unusual woman, Catherine. Even more unusual if you can stick to your plans.'

His smile was so wry that it made Catherine wonder what was behind it before she cut short that thought. She wasn't interested in Matthew as a man but as someone she would be working with. What may or may not have coloured his life in the past didn't concern her, just as her past didn't concern him. They would keep things on a strictly business footing…

'Daddy, you pwomised you'd read me a storwy tonight.'

Catherine looked round when she heard a childish voice and saw a little girl standing in the doorway. She gave Catherine a shy smile as she came into the room and went to stand beside Matthew's chair. She looked very like Matthew with her tumble of sandy blonde curls and deep blue eyes. She was obviously ready for bed, dressed in cosy towelling pyjamas with a ragged old teddy bear clutched in one hand and a well-thumbed book in the other. She gave Catherine a considering look as Matthew put his arm around her.

'I'm Hannah. Who are you?'

'Catherine Lewis.' Catherine smiled although she felt a bit out of her depth. She wasn't used to children except in a professional capacity and wasn't sure what else she should say. However, Hannah had none of her inhibitions, it appeared.

Hannah held out the book she was holding. 'This is my favourite book. Daddy said that he would read it to me but you can do it if he's too busy.'

'Oh…I…um…' Catherine struggled to find an appropriate reply and was saved from having to think one up by Matthew's laughter.

'Oh, no, you don't, you little horror!' He wrapped his arms around the child and hugged her. 'I know what you're up to. Trying to trick poor Catherine into spending the next hour reading to you. You know what the punishment is for that sort of skulduggery!'

'No… Ooh!' Hannah squealed with gleeful laughter when Matthew buzzed her cheek with his chin. 'You're all *pwickly*, Daddy!'

'That's because I need a shave.' He swept the child into his arms and stood up. Hannah wound her arms around his neck and planted a noisy kiss on his cheek.

'I don't really mind if you're all pwickly. I love you anyway.'

It was said with typical childish simplicity yet Catherine felt her eyes fill with sudden tears. She stood up abruptly, using the few seconds it took to push back her chair to gather her composure. She wasn't sure why she'd been so touched to hear Hannah say that. Maybe it was because there was no one in the world who would say the same to her.

The thought was oddly disquieting but, then, the whole evening had been unsettling. All of a sudden, she found herself wondering if this really was the right job for her.

Oh, the surgery was located in the perfect area and the experience she would gain here would be invaluable, but what would be the cost to her personally of working here?

It was another unanswerable question, another uncertainty, and she didn't deal in uncertainties. Her life was structured, planned, assured. That was the way she liked it and how she intended it to continue. She was just debating how to tell Matthew that she wouldn't be taking the job when a woman appeared.

'There you are, Hannah! I wondered where you'd got to.' She turned to Matthew with a rueful smile. 'I'm sorry, darling. I was trying to keep her out of your way because I knew you were busy but she managed to *sneak* out while I was helping Becky with her homework!'

Matthew laughed. 'Don't worry about it, Mum. At least I managed to head her off when she tried to con poor Catherine into reading her a bedtime story.'

The woman turned to Catherine with a chuckle. 'A lucky escape, my dear. You'd have ended up staying the night if you'd fallen for that ploy. With Hannah one story tends to lead to another ad infinitum!'

Mrs Fielding rolled her eyes. She was very like Matthew, with greying sandy blonde hair and bright blue eyes. She had the same wonderfully warm smile and once again Catherine found herself responding to it.

'Obviously a lucky escape,' she replied lightly.

'Oh, don't get overly confident.' Matthew's expression was wry as he set Hannah on her feet. 'This little madam has her ways and means of getting what she wants. So be warned, Catherine. If you're ever working late of an evening and an angelic little face peeps round the door, watch out. She's after your story-telling prowess!'

He seemed to have taken it for granted that she would be accepting the job. Catherine's heart sank when she realised how difficult it was going to be to explain that she was no longer interested in it. She certainly didn't want to go into the whys and wherefores when she wasn't sure that she could give him an acceptable explanation for turning it down.

She decided to tell him simply that she had changed her mind and leave it at that. After all, she didn't owe Matthew Fielding an explanation because it was up to her what she did.

After Mrs Fielding had led a reluctant Hannah away, Catherine saw her chance. 'Dr Fielding, I—'

'Haven't I told you to make it Matt?' He gave a small shake of his head. 'We don't stand on ceremony around here, Catherine, as you'll soon discover—'

He broke off when the telephone rang. Catherine could see that his attention had been distracted but she simply couldn't delay the inevitable any longer. She steeled herself as she said his name for the first time yet it seemed to flow off her tongue with surprising ease.

'Matt, I'm afraid I—'

'Matthew! It's for you, darling.'

Mrs Fielding's voice carried clearly along the corridor and Matt sighed as he headed for the door. 'No rest for the wicked. Sorry, Catherine. I'll be as quick as I can.'

He disappeared before she could say anything and she heard him hurrying along the passage. She looked round uncertainly, sighing when she saw the half-eaten meal on the table. Poor Matthew seemed doomed to go hungry.

She cut off that thought because it really wasn't relevant. Whether or not Matthew Fielding ate wasn't her concern. She went to the door but the corridor was empty. She could hear Matthew's voice coming from the surgery and decided to head that way. It would be easier to tell him that she wasn't going to take the job in the surgery rather than in his kitchen because it would help to put things back on a professional footing. All this chatting over omelettes and coffee didn't do anyone any good!

'Glenda? Hi, it's Matt. Sorry to bother you but I've just had David Marshall's carer on the phone. How was he when you saw him last week?'

Catherine paused when she realised that Matthew must have finished his incoming call and was now making one of his own. She didn't like to interrupt him when it had something to do with a patient. She waited for him to finish, mentally rehearsing what she would say. He was bound to want to know why she didn't want the job but she would just stick to her guns and refuse to discuss her reasons...

'Catherine Lewis...that's right, the one I told you about who had all those wonderful references.'

Catherine hadn't meant to eavesdrop but she couldn't help listening when she heard her name mentioned. She smiled when she heard the remark about her references. She was a good doctor and there was no disputing that.

'How would I sum her up? Well, professionally there's no doubt that she is absolutely first rate and will be able to handle this job without any trouble at all. As for personally...' He paused and his tone was reflective when he continued. 'I suppose the word that springs to mind is vulnerable. Catherine Lewis strikes me as a very vulnerable woman indeed.'

Catherine didn't hear what else he said. She had stopped listening because her mind had seized on that word and wouldn't move forward or back. *Vulnerable.* Was that how Matthew Fielding saw her? Was it true? An hour ago she would have laughed off the suggestion but she couldn't laugh it off now.

'Oh, hi. I'm afraid I have to go out on a call. One of our long-term sick patients has taken a turn for the worse. We use an on-call service after hours normally but this case is a bit different. Motor neurone disease is one of those illnesses you pray someone will find a cure for.'

Matthew was shrugging on his jacket as he came out of the office. He called along the corridor to tell his mother that he was going out then headed towards the front door, obviously expecting Catherine to follow him.

She took a deep breath but her legs felt more than a

little shaky as she trailed after him, her mind even more
so. It was hard to behave naturally as she followed him
out to the car park.

Fortunately, Matthew didn't appear to notice her abstraction as he stopped beside a battered-looking saloon
and unlocked the door. 'Right, I'll expect you on the first
of November, then. You said that you'd be free to start
then, I believe. I'll pop all the paperwork in the post for
you to sign.

'I'm sorry we didn't get much chance to talk. If you
have any questions then just give me a call—after surgery
is usually best. Anyway, thanks for coming tonight,
Catherine. I'm looking forward to us working together.'

He got into the car and started the engine. Catherine
watched in silence as he drove away. She knew she should
have told him that she wouldn't be taking the job but she'd
felt incapable of doing that or anything else.

She got into her car then sat staring through the wind-
screen instead of making any attempt to start the engine.
Vulnerable. It was such an insignificant word to have
scared her the way it had. It was as though everything she
had worked so hard to achieve meant nothing all of a sudden. Matthew Fielding saw her not as the capable, com-
petent woman she had striven so hard to be but as vulnerable. She didn't want to be like that. She wouldn't accept
that she was!

Catherine started the engine and drove out of the surgery. She would prove to him, but, more importantly, she
would prove to herself, that he was wrong.

CHAPTER TWO

VULNERABLE.

On the surface, it wasn't a word that should have applied to the woman seated in front of Catherine's desk. However, it had been on her mind so much in the past weeks that she wasn't surprised when it occurred to her now.

It was the Wednesday of her first week at Brookdale Surgery and she was halfway through morning surgery. Maybe it had been silly to have let Matthew Fielding's comment spur her into taking the job but so far it seemed to be working out extremely well. She had slotted into the new post with surprisingly little trouble. Of course, the fact that the staff at the surgery had been so welcoming had helped enormously. Everyone, from Ann Talbot, their practice nurse, to the two receptionists, Margaret Price and Sharon Goody, had gone out of their way to help her settle in.

As for Matthew, well, he had been nothing less than professional in his dealings with her these past few days. He had been friendly but circumspect, helpful but not overly *familiar* in their exchanges to date. There certainly hadn't been any more offers to share coffee and omelettes, she'd been pleased to note! Catherine was determined their relationship would continue like that. She'd come to Brookdale Surgery to do a job and nothing else.

'So, apart from these dizzy spells, have you experienced any other symptoms, Mrs Hoskins?'

Catherine briskly returned her attention to her patient. Lauren Hoskins was in her thirties, an attractive, well-dressed woman who worked in advertising. The address

on Lauren's records was in a road which had become
highly sought-after in the past few years. A lot of wealthy
couples had chosen to purchase the large Edwardian prop-
erties and refurbish them. However, despite such material
advantages, Lauren exuded a strange aura of vulnerability.
Catherine very much wanted to get to the root of her problems but so far had met with little success.

'Not really.' Lauren smiled wanly. 'Should I have had
other symptoms, Dr Lewis?'

'Not at all,' Catherine replied evenly. 'As I'm not sure
yet what is wrong with you, it certainly isn't possible to
say how you should or shouldn't feel.'

She turned to the computer and checked through the
woman's medical history again. Lauren Hoskins had visited the surgery no less than five times in the past three
months, each time complaining of dizziness. She had seen
Glenda Williams each time and Catherine couldn't fault
the other doctor's thoroughness as she ran through the list
of tests that Lauren had undergone.

'Looking through your records, it appears that you've
been tested for diabetes and high blood pressure. You've
been for an MRI scan to rule out any problems within the
brain, like subdural bleeding, for instance.' Catherine ran
her finger down the list, checking off each test and its
conclusion. 'Dr Williams has eliminated labyrinthitis,
which is often a cause of dizziness, because there was no
sign of inflammation in your inner ears. She has also dis-
counted Ménière's disease because you've not experienced
any deafness or tinnitus—that ringing in the ears which is
symptomatic of the disease. You've also had three pregnancy tests and all have proved negative.'

Catherine glanced at the woman as she came to the end
of the list and noticed how Lauren had quickly averted her
eyes. Had it been the mention of the pregnancy tests which
had caused that reaction? she found herself wondering.

She picked up a pen and pretended to jot down some
notes while she gave herself time to think. Maybe that was

the cause of Lauren's frequent visits to the surgery, the fact that she and her husband had been trying—unsuccessfully—to have a baby? The stress of not conceiving could certainly cause physical symptoms such as dizziness. However, if that were the case, then why was Lauren so reluctant to talk about the problem and seek help? Catherine decided to tread carefully rather than ask her outright.

'I think another pregnancy test would be in order today just to rule out that possibility again.' She took a sample jar out of the drawer and passed it across the desk but Lauren shook her head.

'I'm not pregnant, Dr Lewis. I...I know that for a fact.'

'I see.' Catherine sat back in her chair and studied her quietly. 'Are you and your husband trying for a baby by any chance?'

'No!' Lauren laughed bitterly. 'A baby's the last thing we need at the moment.' She made an obvious effort to collect herself. 'Anyway, that really has nothing to do with why I came today. I just thought—*hoped*—that you might be able to shed some light on these dizzy spells I keep having all the time.'

'I wish I could. However, it does appear that you've had all the tests available, which seems to suggest that the problem isn't anything physical.' Catherine chose her words with care. 'Stress can often be a major contributing factor in a situation like this, Mrs Hoskins. Is there anything worrying you at the moment? Maybe something stressful happening at work or a situation at home which needs resolving?'

'No, of course not! Everything is fine...perfectly fine, both at work and at home! It's just these dizzy spells. That's all.' She stood up abruptly. 'Anyway, I won't waste any more of your time, Dr Lewis. Thank you for seeing me. Good day.'

Catherine hurriedly got up and followed her to the door. Despite what Lauren had said, she sensed there was something very wrong. 'Please, don't rush off, Mrs Hoskins. I'd really like to try and get to the bottom of this problem.'

'It doesn't matter, Dr Lewis. As you said, I've had all the tests available so there doesn't seem much else you can do.'

She quickly left the room. Catherine frowned as she watched her hurrying along the corridor. She couldn't help wondering if she should go after her. It was disquieting to have provoked such a reaction from a patient...

'Problems?'

Matthew had come out of his consulting room and paused when he saw her standing in the corridor. Catherine shrugged, trying to ignore the surge her pulse gave. He had been already hard at work when she had arrived that morning so it was the first she'd seen of him that day. She couldn't help thinking how well the blue of his shirt set off the colour of his eyes, making them sparkle like sapphires.

She hurriedly chased away that fanciful thought before it could take hold. 'I'm not sure.'

'You're not sure?' Matthew grinned. 'Oh, wow, that must be a first!'

Catherine stared at him in bewilderment. 'What do you mean?'

'That I never thought I'd hear you admit there was anything you weren't sure about.' His eyes danced with laughter, making her long to smile back. She managed to curb the urge but it was a struggle all the same.

'I don't know what you mean,' she retorted, turning to go back into her room.

'Don't you?' Matthew followed her inside and propped himself against the doorjamb as he treated her to a considering look. 'So the fact that you've not made any attempt to ask my advice isn't an indication that you prefer to go it alone in the face of whatever adversity?'

His tone couldn't possibly have caused offence, but Catherine knew that he was still making a point. She *hadn't* made any attempt to seek him out even though there had been several occasions when maybe she could have done with his help. Oh, not that there had been anything that she hadn't been able to deal with, of course, but there had been a couple of instances when it would have been helpful to supplement a patient's history with a bit more background information.

It was galling to admit that she had allowed her personal feelings to influence her to such a degree. It had never happened before and she couldn't understand why it had happened now. It was difficult to keep the worry out of her voice when she replied.

'Everything has been fairly straightforward so far.'

'I see. So it wasn't because you were afraid to ask my advice, then?'

'Afraid?'

Her heart surged into her throat as that remark he'd made about her being vulnerable sprang to mind again. She wasn't sure why it bothered her so much. Maybe it was this feeling she had that Matthew could see more than she wanted him to that troubled her. To the world at large she had always presented such a confident front yet she knew that underneath it she wasn't really like that. Inside there was someone completely different, a woman who had fears and uncertainties she had never told anyone about. Did Matthew suspect that? It was that question which worried her most of all.

'Yes.' He sighed. 'I'd hate to think that I came across as unapproachable so if you have a problem, please, don't be afraid to ask my advice. If there is any way that I can help you, Catherine, then you only have to say the word.'

He grinned. 'Although I'm not trying to set myself up as some sort of oracle, you understand, or claim that I have all the answers. There is a hidden agenda to that offer. It means that I can pick *your* brains whenever *I* need help!'

Catherine felt an immediate rush of relief when she realised that she had completely misread the situation. Matthew was simply trying to promote a closer working relationship, not trying to uncover her innermost secrets.

She smiled back, feeling the tension oozing out of her. 'The old two heads are better than one theory?' She laughed when he nodded. 'Well, I'm a firm believer in it, too, so I'll take you up on your offer straight away. What do you know about Lauren Hoskins? I know she's Glenda's patient but has Glenda ever mentioned her?'

'She has, actually. She had a word with me the last time Lauren came to see her because she, too, was puzzled. Evidently, Lauren has had every test under the sun and they've all come back negative.'

'That's right.'

Catherine turned to the computer so she could check through the patient's case history once more. She started nervously when Matthew suddenly appeared at her side and bent to look over her shoulder. He was so close that she could smell the faint aroma of soap which clung to his skin as well as another scent she couldn't quite identify. Her brow furrowed as she tried to work out what it was…

'Baby powder.'

She didn't realise she'd spoken out loud until Matthew looked enquiringly at her. Catherine felt the blush sweep up her face until it felt as though even the roots of her hair must have been glowing.

'Sorry? What did you say?'

'I…um. Nothing.' She managed the weakest of smiles then quickly averted her eyes, focusing on the computer screen as she began to scroll through the list of tests Lauren Hoskins had undergone in the past few months.

'Blood pressure, three times. Diabetes. MRI.' There was the faintest wobble in her voice but she was certain that Matthew wouldn't notice it. He really didn't know her well enough to pick up on something like that. Her confidence returned as he kept his eyes—and his attention—firmly fixed on the screen, seemingly as intrigued as she was by the mystery of why Lauren should be experiencing those dizzy spells all the time.

'Well, it's got me foxed and I don't mind admitting it,' he declared as they came to the end of Lauren's notes. He straightened and Catherine shivered when she was suddenly deprived of the warmth from his body.

Matthew must have noticed her reaction because he frowned. 'If you're cold, turn on the fire. Here, let me do it for you. It can be a bit tricky until you get the knack of lighting the wretched thing.'

He went to the grate to light the old-fashioned gas fire. Catherine looked away as her pulse performed the oddest manoeuvre when she saw how the muscles in his thighs bunched as he crouched down to put a match to the jets. They ignited with a small pop and he quickly adjusted the flames before he stood up.

'It gets really chilly in these rooms with them having such high ceilings,' he observed, dropping the spent match into a misshapen pottery ashtray on the end of the mantelpiece. 'That's why we decided to keep the gas fires when we refurbished the place. Central heating is fine in a modern house but you need a bit of extra heat in these rooms.'

'Yes, I suppose you do,' Catherine replied, struggling to keep any inflection out of her voice. It bothered her that she seemed to notice things about Matthew which she had never been aware of before. When was the last time that she had noticed something like thigh muscles? she thought wonderingly. Probably in anatomy class, the answer came back. And that had been entirely different!

She took a small breath, fighting the feeling of panic which seemed to be closing in on her. She had to deal with this before it got any worse. So Matthew Fielding was a very attractive man, but she had met other attractive men in the past and she would meet many more in the future. She just had to put him into that context.

She wasn't sure if that bit of homespun wisdom would

have an effect but it seemed safer to hope that it would. It also seemed safer to steer the conversation back to what they had been talking about before she had got sidetracked.

'To get back to Lauren Hoskins,' she said, pleased to hear how calm she sounded, a world away from how she really felt. 'Is there anything we might have missed, d'you think?'

'It's possible. Let's go back through everything we know so that we can eliminate all the possibilities one more time.'

Matthew came and sat on the edge of her desk, looking thoughtful as he set his mind to solving the problem. Catherine joined in with relief, feeling easier now that they were concentrating on work. She began listing, and discounting, all the possible causes for Lauren's dizzy spells.

'Blood pressure is fine and her ECG results were excellent. No sign of diabetes or inner ear infections either.'

'She didn't mention anything about feeling sick or vomiting, or that she had trouble with her balance?' Matthew put in.

'Vertigo, you mean?' Catherine shook her head. 'No, I checked that. And there's been no noises in her ears or deafness so we can discount Ménière's. I also checked if the dizzy spells coincided with her menstrual cycle, but they don't. A lot of women get light-headed just before or during menstruation because of hormonal changes.'

'Mmm. I noticed that she's had several pregnancy tests so I assume we can rule out that possibility, too?' Matthew queried.

'Yes. Actually, I offered to do another test today but Lauren was adamant that she couldn't be pregnant.'

Catherine wondered if she should mention the idea she'd had that it might be Lauren's failure to conceive which was causing the problem. She had nothing to base the suspicion on, especially when Lauren had been so quick to deny it, but she couldn't shake off the feeling that it might hold the key to the woman's problems.

'What? I can see that you've thought of something.' Matthew laughed when she looked at him in surprise. 'No, I'm not psychic. You get a sort of broody look on your face whenever something is bothering you!'

Catherine forced herself to smile but the comment had startled her. She had never realised that her expression was so revealing. Unless it was just that Matthew noticed things that other people missed.

The idea unnerved her and she rushed to speak. 'Lauren seemed to get very defensive when I suggested she might be pregnant. I did wonder if there was a problem in that area and if maybe she and her husband had been trying for a baby but not had much success.'

'It's certainly a possibility,' Matthew agreed. 'When you say defensive, though, what do you mean exactly?'

'Oh, just that she denied they were trying for a baby and said that it was the last thing they needed at the moment. I can't explain why it struck me as odd but it did.'

Catherine frowned as she tried to work it out. She heard Matthew sigh and looked at him expectantly. 'What?'

'Just that it isn't easy to help people when they won't tell you what's really wrong. It's one of the curses of working in a middle-class area like this. People can't bear anyone to think that their lives aren't perfect. They seem to see it as some sort of failing on their part, as though they have a duty to maintain the right image.'

Catherine shrugged, more than a little surprised by the observation. 'Most people tend to be like that, surely. They put up a front.'

'To a degree, yes. However, in an area like this, where image and status are so important, it can be a real problem. Maybe Lauren can't have children. Maybe her husband doesn't want them. Who knows? When your life seems perfect to all intents and purposes, you tend to paper over the cracks—hide the bad bits to keep up appearances in front of your friends.' He shrugged. 'The problem is that the bad bits have a way of revealing themselves one way or another.'

'And Lauren's dizzy spells could be an outlet for what is going wrong in her life?' Catherine nodded thoughtfully as she considered that possibility. In a way, it was only what she had been wondering, although Matthew had put a slightly different spin on the idea.

'Yes. If there is no physical cause for her illness then we should try to find a psychological cause.'

'I did think of that. I asked Lauren if there was anything worrying her but once again I have to use that same word and say that she became extremely defensive.' Catherine shook her head. 'I don't know what to do for the best. What about her husband? Do you know anything about him?'

'Not a lot. I've only met him once when they registered with us. He came in for a new-patient check-up.' Matthew shrugged. 'He seemed a pleasant enough chap, a bit full of himself but that's nothing unusual in his line of work.'

'What does he do? I imagine it's something quite high-powered.'

'Peter makes documentaries for television, I believe. I know he was telling me about something he was working on, but I don't recall it ever being broadcast. Although I'm not the best person to ask when it comes to intellectual programmes.'

He grinned. 'My viewing tends to consist mainly of children's programmes. I'm a whiz when it comes to the latest cartoons. I reckon I could win top prize on one of those game shows so long as my specialist subject was the latest cartoon hero to hit the screens!'

Catherine couldn't help laughing. 'A talent like that should be nurtured. Not everyone your age could make such a claim.'

'Don't!' He winced. 'I have a birthday coming up and I'm rather sensitive when it comes to the subject of age.'

It was obvious that he didn't mean a word of it and why

should he? she thought, taking stock of his muscular physique. Matthew was in his prime and many men his age—and younger—would be delighted to be in such excellent shape.

She looked away when she realised where her mind was wandering again. She could hardly believe it had happened a second time. 'On the surface, then, they seem to be a couple who have everything going for them,' she observed, deciding it was safer to stick to work.

'On the surface, yes. But you know as well as I do that it's impossible to judge by appearances.' Matthew frowned. 'I remember Glenda saying one time after Lauren had been to see her that she felt that there was something the woman wasn't telling her.'

'I got that impression, too. How strange. I had this feeling that she *wanted* to tell me what was wrong but that she was…well, afraid to do so.' Catherine sighed. 'I shouldn't have let her rush off like that, should I?'

'You couldn't have stopped her,' he protested, then stopped as Margaret, one of the receptionists, popped her head round the door.

'I hate to disturb you, Matt, but there's a queue outside.' She shot a pointed look at her watch. 'Your eleven o'clock appointment has arrived and your eleven-fifteen…'

'OK. I can take a hint!' Matthew laughed as he got up. 'Anyway, you can blame Catherine this time, not me. She's the culprit.'

'Me?' Catherine echoed in astonishment.

'Uh-huh. I was so fascinated by our conversation that I didn't realise so much time had elapsed. *Ergo*, it's all your fault!'

He gave her a decidedly wicked smile then sauntered out of the room. Catherine hurried to explain when she saw the speculation on Margaret's face. It was obvious the other woman had completely misunderstood Matt's remark.

'Matt…Dr Fielding…meant he was fascinated by a case

we've been discussing,' she gabbled, her tongue tripping over itself in her haste to set matters straight.

'Of course, Dr Lewis.'

Margaret's tone was so bland that the words conveyed exactly the opposite meaning they should have done. Catherine felt heat suffuse her when she realised that the receptionist didn't believe a word she'd said. Did Margaret think that Matt had been wasting his time *chatting her up* instead of seeing to his patients?

It was on the tip of her tongue to assure Margaret that wasn't the case when she suddenly thought better of it. Wasn't there a saying about protesting too much?

'I'll send in your next patient, then, shall I, Dr Lewis?' Margaret asked in the same bland tone.

Catherine nodded because it seemed an awful lot safer. No protestations would pass her lips, no explanations, *nothing*. She wasn't going to give the staff at the surgery anything to gossip about!

'Has she gone?' Matt glanced furtively along the corridor as he sidled back into her room. He treated Catherine to a conspiratorial smile. 'I should have warned you that Margaret is a real termagant when it comes to her beloved appointment system. You dice with death if you mess it up! Anyway, I daren't risk getting in her bad books again so I'll see you after surgery. In the kitchen around twelve-thirty. OK?'

'I...um. Why? I mean, what do you need to see me about?' she demanded, her voice rising by at least an octave. She cleared her throat, striving hard to achieve her usual even tone. 'There isn't much we can do unless Lauren is prepared to tell us what is really wrong with her.'

'There isn't. However, it wasn't Lauren I wanted to talk to you about.'

Matthew cast another wary glance over his shoulder when the door leading from the waiting room opened. 'I need to ask your advice this time, Catherine. The old two heads theory and all that. So, I'll see you in the kitchen later. And don't let Margaret know that I've been in here again or she'll have me shot for dereliction of duty!'

He disappeared and a moment later Catherine heard him greeting his patient with some quip or other. The sound of their laughter was abruptly cut off as his consulting-room door closed.

She took a deep breath, added another for good measure, then went for the hat trick. It didn't work. Maybe Matthew's invitation to meet him in the kitchen hadn't had quite the same ring to it as *Meet me under the clock and I'll wear a red rose*, but it had certainly had an effect on her equilibrium. Making a date...*any kind of a date*...with Matthew Fielding made her feel very vulnerable indeed!

CHAPTER THREE

'HI, THERE! I've made coffee and there's some sandwiches if you're hungry.'

It was twelve thirty-two, precisely. Catherine had checked her watch enough times to know that without having to check it again. The whole time she had been working through the rest of her morning list she had been conscious of the minutes ticking away and bringing the moment for her meeting with Matt ever closer. Maybe it *was* ridiculous to have got herself so worked up, but she hadn't been able to help it. It certainly didn't settle her mind to see the coffee-mugs and plates of sandwiches arranged on the table either. Was this really a work-related meeting, as he'd claimed?

'Sit yourself down. It's just milk, isn't it? You don't take sugar?' Matthew picked up the coffee-pot and brought it over to the table. He put it down on a mat and frowned when he realised she was still standing in the doorway. 'Catherine?'

'I...um. No.' She saw his brows arch and hurriedly tried to get a grip on herself. She wasn't helping the situation by acting like a halfwit.

'No, I don't take sugar,' she explained as much for her own benefit as for his. Keep things simple, Catherine! she chided herself. Stick to the rules. Rule number one was to always maintain her composure. Rule number two was never to mix work with pleasure. Rule number three...

She sighed because there was no point going any further. Rule number three—always to be on her guard—was proving as difficult to adhere to as numbers one and two.

Matthew seemed to have a particular *knack* of sliding past her defences!

She pulled out a chair while Matt filled the mugs with coffee. He shoved the plate of sandwiches towards her then sat down opposite her. 'Try one of these. You won't be disappointed, I promise you. Mum makes the best sandwiches ever.'

Catherine took a sandwich simply because it was easier to comply than refuse. She bit into the moist brown bread and gave a little sigh of pleasure as the flavour of perfectly cooked roast beef and grainy mustard rioted around her taste buds.

'Told you, didn't I?'

The smugness in his voice made her smile despite herself.

'Yes, you did, so you can stop crowing. I don't suppose your mother would like a job? My cooking leaves an awful lot to be desired!'

'No way! You are not poaching her off me. Oh, I might agree to *share* her on the odd occasion but I saw her first, so hands off.' He took a swallow of his coffee then looked enquiringly at her. 'Anyway, haven't you a mother of your own who will take pity on you?'

'No.' Catherine picked up her mug and drank a little of the excellent coffee, using the few seconds it took to remove all expression from her face. 'She died when I was a teenager.'

'Oh, hell! I'm sorry, Catherine.' He reached over the table and squeezed her fingers. 'Me and my big mouth, eh?'

'You weren't to know.'

She eased her hand out of his grasp and picked up her sandwich again but there was a lump the size of Everest in her throat. It was strange because she had thought she had got over the pain of her mother's death a long time ago, but it was as though Matt's sympathy had released all the pent-up emotion. She had a horrible feeling that she was going to cry and hated the thought of him seeing her howling like a baby.

'It must have been hard for you. How old were you when she died?'

His tone was neither overly sympathetic nor totally un-caring this time and Catherine felt her emotions subside to a more manageable level. 'Fifteen. She was killed in a road traffic accident on her way home from work. She was knocked down by a bus while crossing the road.'

'I see. So what happened to you afterwards? Did your father take care of you?'

'No. My parents had divorced a couple of years before the accident happened. My father had moved to California and we'd lost touch,' she explained flatly. She'd had years to come to terms with her father's rejection and it no longer hurt as it had done once upon a time. She shrugged when Matt's expression darkened.

'These things happen, Matt. It's not a big deal. Anyway, as there was no one else to look after me I was put into care and I stayed there until I went to med school. The rest, as they say, is history.'

'So they do, but the trouble with history is that an awful lot gets lost along the way. We remember the key events but so often it's the small, seemingly insignificant mo-ments which have made the biggest impact on us.'

His tone was light enough to be taken as a general ob-servation but Catherine couldn't help wondering if he had realised that she'd left out an awful lot. The idea was far too disturbing so she decided right there and then that she should change the subject. After all, this meeting hadn't been arranged to delve into her past. Matt had said that he needed her advice so maybe it was time she reminded him of that.

'Anyway, enough of all that. Let's get back to what I wanted to speak to you about.'

In the event it was Matt who set the conversation back

on track and she couldn't help feeling irritated at being forestalled. It was galling to feel as though she had no control over what was happening even though he had only done what she'd been intending to do.

'And that was?' she asked coolly.

'David Marshall. He's the patient with motor neurone disease I was called out to see the night you came for your interview, if you remember.'

His tone was bland enough yet she knew without the shadow of a doubt that he had picked up on her irritation. How did he *do* that? she wondered in dismay. How could he read her mind with such apparent ease? She had no idea but it was disturbing to know that he was so receptive to her mood.

'Of course I remember,' she replied curtly. 'You were discussing him on the phone with Glenda.'

She realised her mistake the moment the words were out of her mouth. Matt had had no idea that she'd overheard his conversation that night but would he remember what he'd said about her? Her nerves tightened as she waited for him to answer, but he gave no sign that he was disconcerted by the comment.

'That's right. Both Glenda and I have treated David since he first became ill. We find that it helps him to see different people. He's become increasingly housebound in the last couple of years and misses the contact with the outside world. We alternate our visits so that he gets a bit of variety, so to speak.'

'It must be very difficult for him,' Catherine observed, relieved that he hadn't noticed her slip. 'It's such a cruel illness, especially in its later stages. Those people who suffer from it retain their full mental powers and awareness yet they are locked into a body which won't obey even the most basic commands.'

'Unfortunately, David is fast reaching that point. Until fairly recently he had some mobility and the characteristic muscle tremors weren't too bad. However, the disease seems to have put on a spurt of late and he's now in a wheelchair. It's been a bitter blow for him because he was always so active. He was a rugby player when he was younger, and played for England several times. He also ran his own software company, which was extremely successful.'

'How sad. I take it that he has help—physiotherapy, nursing care, maybe a wife or family who look after him?'

Matt sighed. 'We've managed to get him nursing care and physio, but that's basically it, I'm afraid. He was married but he and his wife got divorced when he first became ill. She couldn't cope with the thought of him becoming disabled, apparently. That's why Glenda and I tend to see him a bit more often than is strictly necessary. There's very little we can do but...'

'But you try to keep up his spirits by visiting him?' Catherine finished for him.

He laughed. 'How did you guess? But you're right, of course. The problem is that David hates the idea of anyone feeling sorry for him. He'd be mortified if he discovered that we don't *need* to visit him so often. We have to be very careful and do all sorts of medical procedures as a cover. I don't think we have another patient on our books who has his blood pressure taken so many times a month!'

'You should be working for MI5!' Catherine declared. 'Between sneaking about when Margaret isn't looking and undertaking clandestine visits to patients, you're absolutely wasted as a GP.'

'I suppose I should get myself one of those trenchcoats and a trilby hat. I need the right clothes to play the part properly, don't I?' Matthew rolled his eyes when she laughed. 'The mind boggles, doesn't it? But leaving all that aside, what I was wondering, Cathy, was whether you'd be willing to help by standing in for Glenda while you're working here.'

'Of course,' she replied immediately because she didn't

want to dwell on how it made her feel to hear him use the diminutive of her name.

She took a deep breath because she couldn't stop herself thinking about it. She couldn't stop herself *feeling* it, in fact. Ripples of warmth seemed to be floating across the surface of her mind, like clouds across a summer sky. Her father had called her Cathy as a child but nobody else had ever done so, mainly because she had discouraged them from using it. The diminutive had always seemed too *familiar* so that the few times her classmates in med school had used it, she had asked them not to. It was strange because it didn't feel wrong to hear Matt using it now. Admittedly, it had generated all sorts of feelings but it didn't feel *wrong*…

'Is that a problem?'

She started when she realised that she hadn't heard a word that he'd said. 'Pardon?'

There was a huskiness in her voice which she had never heard in it before. She noticed it immediately but so, too, did Matt. Catherine felt her heart race when he suddenly got up from the table. He went to the sink and turned on the tap, keeping his back towards her so that she couldn't see his expression. And when he spoke his voice was even huskier than hers had been so that she shivered when she felt the uneven timbre strumming along her nerves.

'I was just saying that Glenda and I usually visit David outside working hours.'

He turned off the tap and she saw his shoulders rise and fall as he took a deep breath. Catherine had no idea what he was hoping to achieve by it but it definitely didn't do anything for *her* dilemma. Witnessing the struggle Matt was having to stay focused certainly didn't ease her mind.

'I know it's an imposition to ask you to see a patient in your free time so just say if you don't want to do it, Cath…'

'It's fine. Really!' She gave the most inane laugh ever but it was better than hearing Matt call her by that seduc-

tive little name again. Pushing back her chair, she hastily
got to her feet. 'I don't mind in the least going to see him
out of surgery hours, really I don't.'

'That's very kind of you.'

Matt had himself under control again and she felt her
knees go weak with relief when he turned and she saw that
his face held nothing more than approval. 'David is down
for a visit tomorrow afternoon, as it happens. We usually
pop in to see him on our free afternoons as it's easier that
way. I like to be at home with the children of an evening.
It's hard to find enough time to spend with them as it is.'

'It must be,' she agreed, as though bringing up a family
was something she knew all about. Quite frankly, she
couldn't begin to imagine how hectic his life must be,
taking care of his daughters, being, in effect, both mother
and father to them. It should have made her see how lucky
she was to have only herself to worry about and yet for
some reason she didn't feel lucky when she thought about
it. There was no one for *her* to go home to after work,
nobody to worry about or who would worry about her—
nobody to love.

She blinked and her mind miraculously cleared. What
on earth was she thinking? She liked her life exactly the
way it was and having a family wasn't something she had
ever planned on doing!

'It isn't a problem,' she said firmly, relieved to be back
on familiar ground. 'You can put me down for a visit tomorrow afternoon, if you like.'

'Great! That's a weight off my mind, I can tell you. I
had visions of having to forfeit my afternoons off for the
next twelve months. It would have been a nightmare because I can barely find the time to fit everything in as it
is.' He grimaced. 'Heaven knows how I'm going to cope
when Mum goes to Canada. It doesn't bear thinking
about!'

'Canada!' Catherine exclaimed. 'Good heavens, when is
she planning on going there?'

'The middle of December. My sister, Cheryl, is expecting her first baby, you see, so Mum is going to stay with her until after Christmas. It's taken me ages to persuade Mum that she should go but I know how much she wants to be with Cheryl. It isn't fair that she should miss out because she feels she should stay here to help me look after the girls.'

'How will you manage without her, though? Surely it won't be easy, looking after the children as well as working?' Catherine queried, thinking what a massive understatement that was. Just thinking about the logistics of caring for a family whilst doing a full-time job filled her with dread.

'I've no idea.' Matt grinned when she stared at him. 'I shall just have to muddle through, I suppose. Fortunately, Becky is old enough to look after Hannah for an hour or so when they get home from school, so I shall have to try to be more efficient and get through my evening list on time. It should earn me a few brownie points with Margaret, if nothing else.'

'Get through your list on time?' Catherine repeated. 'I'll believe that when it happens.'

'Are you implying that I'm tardy, Dr Lewis?' he demanded, glowering at her.

'Not at all. You aren't tardy, Dr Fielding. You're downright late!'

She gave him a teasing smile which wavered when she saw the expression on his face. There was laughter there, of course, but along with that there was something else...

She turned away, her heart racing as she tried to come to terms with what she had just witnessed, but it wasn't easy to deal with the idea that Matt was attracted to her. She tried to tell herself that it wasn't true but it was pointless lying after what she'd just seen. Matt regarded her not just as a colleague but as an attractive woman whom he wanted to get to know better. Whilst part of her rejoiced at the idea, another part flatly rejected it.

'I'd better get sorted out,' she murmured, conscious of his gaze following as she went to the door. 'I've quite a few house calls to do this afternoon and I don't want to be late getting back for evening surgery.'

'Of course not, but don't work too hard, will you, Cathy?'

Catherine didn't say anything as she hurriedly left. She went straight to her room and picked up the pile of call slips Margaret had left for her. She needed to check through them so she could put them in order of priority.

The pieces of paper fell from her hands but she didn't even notice. All she could think about was Matt's voice when he had said her name just now: Cathy. Maybe the name could be applied to her but it certainly didn't reflect the person she was or, rather, the one she *tried* to be. Cathy was the name of the woman she kept hidden away inside her.

That person didn't need to be in control all the time. She didn't set boundaries or live by any rules. Cathy didn't have ambitions or goals to achieve. She was just a warm, caring, *loving* woman who longed to be loved in return; a woman who would do a job because it was the job she wanted to do; a woman who would love a man because— rightly or wrongly—he was the man she loved.

How Catherine *envied* that woman. How she *feared* her because it was the Cathys of this world who found true happiness yet the risks they took to achieve it were just too great. She had always known that she could be either Cathy or Catherine but that she couldn't be both, and she had made her decision a long time ago which it had to be. Just because Matthew Fielding seemed to possess this power to disturb her, it wasn't a good enough reason to start having second thoughts.

Catherine picked up the slips of paper. She quickly sorted them into order then left the surgery. It felt good to be back on course once more.

*   *   *

'Matthew, it's me, Catherine. Look, I'm sorry to phone you like this but I seem to have a bit of problem.'

Catherine glanced nervously over her shoulder when she heard a noise behind her but it was only a rusty old can being blown along the pavement by the wind. She huddled closer to the wall, wishing that she was safely back at the surgery.

It was almost four o'clock and she had never expected to still be doing house calls at that time of the day, but things hadn't gone according to plan. A number of the calls she'd made that afternoon had taken far longer than she'd anticipated so that she'd been running late even before she'd arrived at the block of flats on the very edge of their catchment area. In contrast to the more prosperous streets she had driven through that afternoon, this whole area was very run-down. Most of the flats seemed to have been boarded up and there were mounds of rubbish strewn across the street. Although there was nobody about, she couldn't deny that she felt extremely edgy.

'What's wrong?' Matthew's voice sharpened in concern and for some reason she found herself relaxing. It was strangely comforting to know that he was worried about her.

'Would you believe that I'm lost?' she replied, trying to damp down the warm glow that had flooded through her.

'I'd find it rather hard, I have to admit.'

He laughed and she had a sudden mental image of him sitting at his desk in his office. His blue eyes would be full of laughter and his mouth would be curled into that wonderful smile which never seemed to be far from his lips...

'Getting lost doesn't strike me as something you do very often, Cathy.'

The warmth inside her increased tenfold when he called her by the diminutive again. Catherine fought to control it by focusing on the problem at hand.

'It isn't, and I really can't understand what's gone

wrong this time,' she said briskly. 'There's only one street
with this name according to my map. Is it possible that
Margaret could have given me the wrong address?'

'Well, it's possible, I suppose, although I have to say
that it's highly unlikely. Margaret is a stickler for detail
whenever anyone requests a home visit.' Matt sounded
puzzled. 'Tell me where you are and I'll check it out.'

'Thanks.' Catherine rattled off the name and address that
had been written on the call slip.

'Got it. Hang on a sec while I check the files,' he instructed. 'The patient's name doesn't seem to ring any
bells, I have to confess.'

There was a soft thud as he put the receiver down.
Catherine clamped the cellphone against her ear as she
waited for him to come back. She wasn't normally a nervous person but there was something decidedly unsettling
about standing in the middle of the deserted street. It was
a huge relief when Matt came back on the line a few seconds later.

'I've got the file right here in front of me and the information you have is correct. We have Mrs Grimes listed
as living at number forty-two Ansell Heights.'

'Then I'm not sure what's happened,' Catherine admitted, hoping Matt couldn't tell how nervous she felt. 'I must
have knocked at least a dozen times, but I couldn't get an
answer.'

'That's strange. According to our records, Mrs Grimes
has lived there for some time. She must be in her seventies
now and the last time we saw her at the surgery was just
over three years ago. She's one of Glenda's patients, which
explains why I don't remember her.'

There was a touch of impatience in his voice but
Catherine knew she wasn't responsible for it. He was an-
noyed with himself for not being able to recall the patient
in question.

'You can't remember every patient who's registered
with the practice,' she pointed out.

'Hmm, s'pose not.' He gave a rueful laugh. 'How did you know what I was thinking?'

How indeed? It was a good question and one she had no intention of answering. 'A lucky guess,' she replied shortly, refusing to dwell on how easily she had latched onto his thoughts. 'Anyway, thanks for checking the address for me. I'll give it one last shot then call it a day. Maybe Mrs Grimes felt better and went out, forgetting that she'd asked for a home visit.'

'It's possible but I think I'll have a word with Social Services to see if they've had any dealings with her recently. I'd hate to think she might be too ill to answer the door.'

'Good point,' Catherine agreed. 'I'll check back with you if I can't get a reply this time and we'll take it from there.'

'Do that. I'm here if you need me, Cathy. Just give me a call.'

'I will.'

Catherine sighed as she slipped the phone into her pocket, wondering if she should ask Matt not to keep calling her Cathy. She didn't want to cause a fuss but it might be better to make her feelings clear. Of course, the other alternative was to ignore it…

Oh, yeah! a small voice jeered. So she could ignore him calling her *Cathy*, could she?

Her mouth pursed because she really wasn't used to behaving in this ambivalent fashion. Normally, she wouldn't have hesitated about making her feelings plain so it was galling to find herself debating the issue. What was it about Matt that made even the simplest decision so difficult?

She had no more idea what the answer was to that question than she had to so many others that seemed to have arisen of late so she put it out of her mind as she went back inside the building and made her way to the fourth floor. She rapped on the door and almost leapt out of her skin when a querulous voice answered from inside.

'Who's there? What do you want?'

'It's Dr Lewis, Mrs Grimes. From Brookdale Surgery.'

'Lewis? I don't know any doctor by the name of Lewis. You get away from here. Go on. Leave me alone!'

Catherine frowned when she heard the panic in the old lady's voice. The poor soul sounded really terrified and she couldn't understand why she should be so afraid.

'I'm new at the surgery, which is why you won't have heard of me. I only started working there on Monday, in fact. I'm replacing Dr Williams while she's away on leave.'

She carried on in the same reassuring vein when the old lady didn't reply. 'There's really nothing to be frightened about, Mrs Grimes. I just want to check that you're all right so won't you, please, open the door?'

Catherine held her breath, hoping that her reassurances would have the desired effect. She heaved a sigh of relief when she heard bolts being drawn before a wrinkled face peered round the door.

'Are you sure you're from the surgery? You ain't one of that other lot, are you?'

'No.' Catherine shook her head although she had no idea what the old lady had meant. 'I'm one of the doctors from Brookdale Surgery. Here's my identity card.'

She passed the plastic wallet containing her ID through the opening and after a moment the old lady opened the door properly.

'I suppose you'd better come in.'

'Thank you.' Catherine followed the old lady into a cluttered sitting room. Every surface was piled high with old newspapers and magazines and she paused while she tried to find somewhere to put her case. She finally spotted a gap on the end of the dining table and went towards it.

'Mind you don't knock anything over!' Mrs Grimes warned her. 'My Alfred was most particular about keeping his papers in order, said that he could lay his hand on whatever he wanted, he did.'

'Don't worry, Mrs Grimes. I'll be careful,' Catherine assured her, thinking that Alfred must have been a genius if he could perform that feat. If there was any kind of filing system to the papers then it certainly wasn't apparent!

She put her bag down then went and perched on the edge of the settee. 'Now, would you like to tell me what's wrong, Mrs Grimes?'

'This.' The old lady lifted her skirt to reveal a large area of reddened flesh on her bony thigh.

Catherine frowned in concern. 'That looks very nasty. How did it happen?'

'It was my Timmy, you see. He jumped onto my knee when I was having my breakfast and I spilled my cup of tea. Hurt quite a lot it did, which is why I called you.'

'I'm sure it must have done,' Catherine agreed, getting up to fetch a pair of gloves from her case. She knelt down beside the old lady and gently examined the scald, which extended from the top of Mrs Grimes's left thigh almost to her knee. The skin had blistered and some of the blisters had broken and were oozing serum. Catherine frowned when she saw that bits of wool from the old lady's skirt had stuck to the open wounds. She would need to clean up the whole area before she could dress it.

'So who's Timmy, then? Is he your dog?' she asked hoping to distract the old lady's attention. Although the scald wasn't severe enough to warrant hospitalisation, it was bound to be painful.

'He's a cat, a big old thing who's past his sell-by date. A bit like me, in fact!' Mrs Grimes gave a cackling laugh and Catherine chuckled.

'Well, he's a naughty cat if this is an example of the trouble he causes.'

'That's as maybe, but I wouldn't give him up for anything.' Mrs Grimes's tone was belligerent all of a sudden. 'He's all I've got now that my Albert is dead. I know to some folks he's only a cat but to me he's family. We didn't have children, me and Albert—we weren't blessed that way—but we always had a cat and Timmy is the best one of them all. They won't make me move from here until they find me some place where I can take my Timmy, and I've told them that!'

'They?' Catherine repeated. 'Do you mean the council?'

'Council. Social Services. They're all the same to me. It don't really matter what they call themselves. They come in here, telling me what I can and can't do, saying that they're very sorry, Mrs Grimes, but you can't take your cat with you but at least you'll have a nice new flat to live in so don't worry.' The old lady sucked in an indignant breath. 'Told them straight, I did—if I can't take Timmy then I'm going nowhere. I don't care if I'm the last one left in the whole building because I'm not moving without him!'

Catherine sighed as she put down the tweezers she'd been using. It explained why the old lady was still living in the block of flats when most of the other tenants had left. Mrs Grimes had refused to be parted from her beloved pet.

She got up and went to her case for some Tulle Gras dressings. The dressings were impregnated with antibiotic and would minimise the risk of infection, which was one of the biggest problems associated with this kind of injury. She carefully dressed the old lady's leg, thinking how wrong it was that someone as vulnerable as this should be treated in such a cavalier fashion.

'Surely the council could find you a place to live where you could take Timmy? There must be a lot of people like you, who have pets they don't want to be parted from.'

Mrs Grimes shrugged. 'That's what I keep telling them but they take no notice. They seem to think they can push me around because I'm too old to fight them...' She broke off when a huge ginger-coloured tom-cat appeared. 'Here he is now. Come on Timmy, darlin'. Come to your mum.'

Catherine laughed when the cat stalked across the room

and sat down beside the old lady's chair. 'He seems to understand what you say to him, doesn't he?'

'Course he does! Understands every word, don't you, sweetheart? That's why he's such good company. Why, if I didn't have my Timmy to look after then there'd be no reason to get up of a morning. He's what keeps me going.'

And yet some faceless officials were trying to force the poor soul into giving up the animal. Catherine felt a sudden spurt of anger at such high-handed officialdom. As she cleared up, she found herself wondering if there was anything she could do to help the old lady. Normally, she wouldn't have dreamt of getting involved with a patient's housing problems, but Mrs Grimes's plight had touched her. Maybe a phone call to the local housing office would garner some positive results?

She made a note to contact them the following day although she decided not to mention it to Mrs Grimes in case she raised her hopes unnecessarily. She locked her case and picked it up.

'Your leg should feel a bit better now, Mrs Grimes, but you're going to need the dressings changed so I'll ask Ann Talbot, our practice nurse, to call round to see you.'

'I'd rather you came, Doctor. I know who you are now so what's the point in me having to get used to someone else?' Mrs Grimes glanced at the cat. 'And Timmy knows you now as well.'

Catherine laughed. 'In that case, it does seem silly to involve Ann, doesn't it? Very well, Mrs Grimes, I'll call round again tomorrow afternoon to check how you are.'

'I'll be here, Doctor,' Mrs Grimes assured her. 'I don't get out much nowadays. Most of the time the lift isn't working and it's a bit of a struggle up and down all those stairs.'

The old lady started to get up but Catherine shook her head. 'No, you stay there. I can let myself out. I'll see you tomorrow, Mrs Grimes. And you, too, Timmy.'

Catherine left the flat and made her way down to the

street. It was pitch black outside and she groaned when she realised just how late she was going to be for surgery. The evening rush hour would have started by now and that would add even more time to her journey…

'Everything OK?'

She whirled round and felt her heart thump when she spotted Matthew leaning against his car. 'What are you doing here?'

'Waiting for you, of course.' He glanced at his watch as he straightened and walked towards her. 'You had another thirty seconds before I came to find you.'

'You were coming to find me?' she repeated blankly. 'But why?'

'Because I was worried about you.' He smiled at her, his eyes gently mocking her. 'Naturally.'

Naturally? Was it really a foregone conclusion that he should worry about her? Catherine knew that she should stop right there and not allow herself to go any further. The fact that Matt had been concerned enough to come all this way to find her was more than enough to contend with, without adding anything else to the equation.

How long had it been since anyone had cared about her this much? she thought wonderingly, then quickly blanked out the thought because it made her feel far too vulnerable to think about it.

'I appreciate your concern,' she said stiffly, trying to hide how mixed up she felt. She didn't want Matt to feel responsible for her but she'd be a liar if she tried to claim that it didn't feel good to know that he cared. 'However, you needn't have worried because I was fine.'

'That's good to hear but I couldn't stop myself worrying, Cathy.'

He touched her lightly on the arm and even through the thickness of her winter jacket she could feel the comforting heat of his hand. It was a relief when he released her as he turned to look along the street because she knew just how tempting it would be to let his hand remain on her arm. When Matt touched her like that she felt safe, and it was such an unexpected feeling that it scared her. It was an effort to concentrate because the thought of ever relying on anyone other than herself was more than she could bear.

'After you rang off I suddenly remembered reading that this whole area was scheduled for demolition. I was afraid that someone had sent you on a wild-goose chase—used Mrs Grimes's name and address to get you here under false pretences. I decided that it wasn't worth taking any risks and that I would check that you were all right.'

'And as you can see, I'm fine.' Catherine summoned a smile, determined not to let him see how rattled she was. She had decided a long time ago that she would never put herself in the same position her mother had been in. She would never, ever allow anyone to let *her* down!

'I hadn't realised the whole street was due to come down,' she said, drawing strength from the thought. 'It makes it even more imperative that something should be done to help Mrs Grimes. It's a disgrace that a woman her age should be left in a place like this.'

'I agree. Why hasn't the council rehoused her? Did she say?'

'Apparently, she refused to move because they wouldn't let her take her cat.'

'Typical heavy-handed bureaucracy!' Matthew snorted in disgust. 'So what are we going to do about it?'

We? Since when had this become his concern? Catherine wondered. He seemed to have taken it for granted that they would work together and she wasn't sure how she felt about it. To move from *I* to *us* mightn't be a very big step in terms of conjugating the verb, but it was a gigantic leap by her terms.

'*I* thought I would contact the housing office tomorrow,' she explained, delicately emphasising the personal pronoun.

'Fine, then *I* shall get onto Social Services and see what they have to say.'

Matthew gently mocked her but she knew there was no point trying to stop him. He'd made up his mind that he intended to stand shoulder to shoulder with her in this battle and nothing would stop him seeing it through.

'Fine.' Catherine turned away before he could see her expression. Maybe it was because she had grown used to facing the world alone that made her feel so emotional at the thought of Matt supporting her. She no longer felt completely on her own and it was a strange feeling, one she really didn't know how to deal with. It was a relief to get back into her car and close the door because it made her feel in control once more.

Matt tapped on the window and she reluctantly wound it down a couple of inches. 'Do you want to follow me back to the surgery? I know a short cut, although we're still going to be extremely late.' He pulled a face. 'I don't know if I can cope with Margaret telling me off *twice* in one day. D'you think she'll make me write out one hundred times, "I must not keep my patients waiting"?'

Catherine laughed because she couldn't help it. His expression was just so comical. 'Only one hundred times? I think you're being a bit optimistic. More like *two* hundred times, I'd say!'

'Don't!' He groaned as he flexed his fingers. 'Oh, I can feel a severe case of writer's cramp setting in already! Still, the consolation is that you'll be in the doghouse with me. We can write out our lines together.'

He gave her a last, cheeky grin then got into his car. Catherine started the engine then waited for Matt to set off. He stuck his arm out of the window and waved then led the way up the street, monitoring his speed so that she had no difficulty keeping up as he wove through a complicated network of back streets.

Catherine grimaced as she followed him along the route. She would never have found this by herself! They came to a junction with the main road and she had to stop although Matt managed to cross over. She saw him pull in to wait for her and felt a wave of warmth encompass her. It felt so good to be looked after like this—too good, in fact.

The feeling of warmth abruptly faded as it struck her how easy it would be to rely on him. Matt was that kind of a person—reliable, trustworthy, dependable. He was also a lot of other things as well, like handsome and fun, kind and caring, and that made him even more dangerous. The Matthew Fieldings of this world weren't for her. There could be no half-measures with a man like Matt, no compromises. If he loved a woman it would be with his whole heart and without reservation. That he would expect the same from the woman concerned went without question but Catherine had no intention of giving any man that much power over her.

Her heart was suddenly heavy as she crossed the junction and followed Matt's car as he set off again. She might be content to let Matt lead her back to the surgery but she must never let him lead her astray.

CHAPTER FOUR

ALTHOUGH Matthew's short cut had helped, they were still fifteen minutes late by the time they arrived back at the surgery. Matt went straight inside while Catherine was parking her car, obviously wanting to reassure the reception staff that they hadn't been deserted.

Catherine shrugged off her jacket as she hurriedly followed him into the surgery. The waiting room was packed and she smiled apologetically at the two receptionists as she passed their desk.

'I am so sorry I'm late! I got held up, I'm afraid.'

'Think nothing of it, Dr Lewis. We're used to it, aren't we, Sharon?' Margaret cast a world-weary look at the younger receptionist, who grinned.

'But it really isn't like me,' Catherine insisted, not wanting them to get the wrong idea. 'I'm always so punctual normally.'

'If being late the odd time or two is your only sin then I think we can live with that.'

Catherine spun round when she heard Matt's voice. He treated her to such a warm smile that her heart skipped a beat. 'I think we're very lucky to have you working here, Catherine. Wouldn't you agree, ladies?'

Margaret gave him an old-fashioned look. 'As you say, Dr Fielding,' she agreed archly.

Catherine felt a wave of colour rush to her face when she saw the look the receptionists exchanged. It didn't take a genius to work out what they were thinking, she thought as she hastily excused herself and went to her room. It was obvious that Margaret and Sharon didn't believe Matt's appreciation was solely for her professional skills!

54

She took a deep breath before she pressed the buzzer to summon her first patient. She had to put thoughts like that out of her head while she concentrated on work. However, it wasn't easy to dismiss the thought that Matt was interested in her when it could cause so many problems.

Mercifully, there weren't any really difficult cases to deal with that evening. Most of the people she saw seemed to be suffering from the usual coughs and colds which were the staple of any GPs working day. There were also a couple of patients with asthma—always a problem for people living in the city and constantly breathing in pollutants. The worst case was a boy called Benjamin King, who'd been treated at the surgery for a number of years. Benjamin was just thirteen and Catherine could see he was extremely distressed when he and his mother came into the room.

'Sit on the couch, Benjamin,' she instructed, raising the back support so that the boy could make himself comfortable. 'Now, I want you to try and relax. I know it's scary when you can't breathe properly but there's no need to worry. I'll make sure that you're OK.'

Catherine smiled reassuringly at the boy as she monitored his breathing, listening to the wheezing sound he was making as he struggled to force oxygen into his lungs. Asthma attacks could be triggered by any number of things, from exercise to dust mites, but the effect they had was always terrifying for the sufferer. As the airways became inflamed they also narrowed, drastically reducing the amount of air that could flow into and out of the lungs. The patient would then start to panic and the situation would deteriorate.

Catherine was anxious to avoid that happening now. Unhooking the oxygen mask, she slipped it over Benjamin's nose and mouth. 'Now, I want you to take nice slow breaths. One…and two…and three…'

The boy's breathing gradually steadied as he began to

calm down. 'That's great!' she declared. 'Just keep on like that and you'll be fine.'

She turned to the boy's anxious mother. 'Has Benjamin been taking his medication as per instructions? I see that he's been prescribed sodium cromoglycate as an anti-inflammatory plus salbutamol as a bronchodilator.'

'Yes, he never misses his medication. I make sure of that.' Sandra King managed a wobbly smile but Catherine could tell how much of a strain she was under. 'And I nag Benjie to death about making sure he always has his inhaler with him!'

'That's what mothers are for,' Catherine replied lightly. 'Do you know what triggered the attack tonight? I see from Benjamin's records that he's been fairly well of late.'

'He has, but, then, it's usually the case, isn't it, Doctor? Just when you start to think that maybe he's getting better, something happens.' Sandra sighed. 'As to what triggered it off tonight, well, it could have been what he was doing at school this afternoon.'

'Oh, what was that?' Catherine took another look at Benjamin and was pleased to see that his breathing had improved considerably.

'He went on a geography field trip—spent the afternoon mapping out the area around his school to show where the shops and the park and things like that are. It might have been breathing in all those traffic fumes which did the damage because he wasn't too good when he came home from school and it just got steadily worse from there.'

'I expect you're right. Traffic pollution is a huge problem in the city.' Catherine bent and carefully removed the oxygen mask from the boy's face. 'Feeling any better now?'

'A bit,' Benjamin mumbled.

He was at an age where he must resent having to constantly monitor the things he could do, she thought. Asthma sufferers were taught to avoid activities which might trigger an attack and, whilst it might be easy for an adult to accept such restrictions, it was difficult for a child, as Benjamin soon made clear.

'I wish I didn't have this rotten illness! It isn't fair. None of my friends have asthma and they can do all kinds of things that I can't!'

'It must be hard, Benjamin,' she agreed. 'However, it's been some time since you had a really bad attack so maybe you're starting to grow out of them. A lot of people stop having attacks as they get older.'

'That's what Dr Fielding said the last time he saw you, didn't he, Benjie?' Sandra smiled encouragingly at her son. 'And once your dad starts this new job then you'll probably feel loads better. Just think, we'll be living by the sea by Christmas and it's bound to be a lot cleaner living there than in the middle of this dirty old city!'

'But I won't have my friends there, will I?' Benjamin declared mutinously, obviously not happy about the forthcoming move. 'It's going to be really *boring*!'

Catherine sighed as she wrote out a repeat prescription then saw Benjamin and his mother out. There were no easy answers to some problems and, where they involved children, that seemed to make things even more complicated. That immediately reminded her of what Matt had told her about his mother going away. She couldn't help worrying how he was going to manage even though it didn't have anything to do with her. How strange.

There were still a few more patients to see after the Kings left so it was gone seven before she finished. She gathered up the files and took them through to the office for filing. Although they used a computer system, like a lot of practices they also kept a manual back-up of data for each patient.

The old belt-and-braces theory, Catherine thought wryly as she popped the files into the tray. Computers were all well and good but you knew where you were with paper, and it didn't sprout those wretched little gremlins which computers were so prone to.

Margaret and Sharon had already left so she switched off the light then paused when she saw Matt coming down the corridor with an elderly woman hanging onto his arm. He stopped when they reached her.

'I'm just going to see Mrs Hargreaves across the road, Catherine. It's late-night shopping tonight and the traffic is horrendous.' He raised his voice so the old lady could hear him. 'This is Dr Lewis, Mrs Hargreaves. She'll be working here while Dr Williams is on maternity leave.'

'Oh, nice to meet you, dear. Lovely news about Dr Williams expecting, isn't it? Have you got any children?'

Catherine followed Matt's lead and raised her voice. 'No. I'm not married, Mrs Hargreaves.'

'That don't seem to make much difference nowadays!' the old lady retorted. 'Walking out with someone, then, are you?'

'Walking out?' Catherine repeated uncertainly.

'What Mrs Hargreaves means is are you dating anyone, Catherine?' Matt's tone was bland enough yet Catherine felt herself blushing. She couldn't help feeling self-conscious about having to discuss her private life in front of him.

'Um…no, actually. I'm not going out with anyone at the moment.'

'Eh? What was that? You'll have to speak up, dear. I don't hear so well as I used to.'

Mrs Hargreaves cupped a blue-veined hand to her ear and Catherine's blush deepened even though she knew it was silly to feel embarrassed. What possible difference could it make to Matt whether or not she was dating some-one?

'I don't have a boyfriend, Mrs Hargreaves.' She shook her head to emphasise the negative and the old woman smiled.

'Oh, I see. Still, there's plenty of time to find yourself a nice man.' She patted Matthew's arm. 'You wouldn't have to look very far neither. You couldn't find anyone better than Dr Fielding, if you want my advice.'

'That sounds very much as though you are matchmaking, Mrs Hargreaves.'

Thankfully, Matt stepped in and spared Catherine from having to think up a reply. He wagged an admonishing finger at the old lady. 'Shame on you for embarrassing poor Dr Lewis like that!'

'Don't know why she should be embarrassed when I was only speaking the truth, but I'll not say another word more on the subject if you don't want me to,' the old lady replied stoutly. 'Anyway, come along, then. Let's be off. I want to get home to watch the telly and you've got them youngsters to see to. That's another reason why you should be thinking about finding yourself a wife. Those kiddies need a mother!'

'I give up!' Matthew shook his head in despair. 'You really are incorrigible.' He turned to Catherine and grimaced. 'You must think I'm a really sad case if my patients are trying to marry me off.'

She managed a weak smile. 'Not at all.'

'Good, I'm glad to hear it, although you could have tried to sound a *bit* more convincing!'

His smile told her that he was joking but Catherine decided it might be wiser not to say anything. She didn't feel any more comfortable about discussing Matt's love life than she'd felt about discussing her own. Matt obviously took the hint because he smoothly changed the subject.

'Would you mind hanging on here until I get back, Catherine? I don't have my keys with me and I don't want leave the surgery unlocked. I should only be a few minutes.'

'Don't worry. I'll wait,' she assured him.

'Thanks.'

Matt smiled his thanks then continued along the corridor, shortening his stride to accommodate the old lady's slower pace. It was typically thoughtful of him to go out of his way to help her, Catherine thought. His kindness was an intrinsic part of his nature and one of the things she liked most about him.

She frowned, somewhat surprised by that thought. She rarely formed opinions about the people she worked with, mainly because they never aroused her interest to any extent. However, there was something about Matt which appealed to her on many different levels. She certainly wasn't indifferent to him.

The idea was oddly unsettling. Catherine found herself trying to work out why Matt should have this effect on her as she made her way along the corridor. She paused outside his room then slowly went inside. Maybe she would find a clue to explain the mystery in here?

She looked around, taking stock of all the usual fitments she would have expected to see in any doctor's consulting room. The mahogany desk and chairs were very similar to the ones in her own room, ditto the green leather examination couch and screen. The shelves and cupboards which lined the walls held all the usual paraphernalia needed in the course of a working day. In fact, everything in the room seemed to be of a purely functional nature and did little to solve her problem.

She turned to leave then stopped when she caught sight of a framed photograph on the desk. She picked it up and studied it curiously. Matt was instantly recognisable even though the picture must have been taken several years ago if the baby he was holding was Hannah. The other child must be his elder daughter, Catherine decided, although the little girl didn't look anything like Matt with that long dark hair and deep brown eyes. Maybe she favoured her mother more?

'Excuse me, but do you know where my dad is?'

Catherine swung round, feeling rather guilty about being caught snooping. She immediately recognised the girl who was standing in the doorway as the child in the photograph even though she was several years older now.

'Your father is helping a patient across the road,' she explained, quickly putting the photograph back in its place. 'He shouldn't be very long, though.'

'Oh.'

Catherine's brows rose when she heard the disappointment in her voice. 'That sounded ominous. Problems?'

The girl sighed. 'I'm stuck on my French homework. Gran usually helps me but she's gone to the cinema tonight with Aunt Bet...she's my *great*-aunt really but she hates me calling her that...so I wanted Dad to help me instead. I'm Becky, by the way.'

'And I'm Catherine Lewis, the new doctor who's standing in for Glenda.'

'Oh, I already guessed that. Hannah told me all about you. She said that you were really nice and had promised to read her a story...' Becky stopped and looked hopefully at her. 'I don't suppose you speak French, do you? Maybe you could help me seeing as my dad isn't here?'

'Your father shouldn't be very long,' Catherine began, then stopped when she saw Becky's crestfallen expression. She wasn't *that* old that she couldn't remember how long even ten minutes had felt when she'd been a child.

'All right, I'll give it a go. But don't expect too much, will you? My French is *very* rusty!'

'Cool! And your French can't be as rusty as Dad's because you aren't *nearly* as old as he is! I'll just fetch my books.'

Catherine chuckled as Becky hurried away. She would love to see Matt's reaction to that comment after what he'd said earlier in the day about having a birthday coming up! Becky came back a few minutes later and put the books on the desk.

'It's this bit here I'm stuck on. I've got to translate it into French and I don't know if I've got the verb right.'

Catherine looked at what she had written and quickly spotted the problem. 'I think it should be *voudrais* but we'd better check just to be sure.'

She and Becky were soon engrossed in the intricacies of French verbs so that neither of them realised that Matt had returned. It was only when she happened to look up that Catherine saw him standing in the doorway. There was the oddest expression on his face, a kind of wistful longing that filled her with an unexpected feeling of tenderness. She wanted to put her arms around him and hold him close, promise him that she would do everything in her power to make him happy, but how could she do that? She couldn't take the risk of becoming involved in his life because of the effect it could have on her future plans.

'Here's your father now, Becky,' she said, struggling to keep the ache out of her voice. She wasn't sure why it was so difficult to draw back when she'd found it the easiest thing in the world to do in the past. There had been few occasions when she had felt any desire to get close to someone, but she couldn't deny that she felt it now. It scared her because she knew just how dangerous it was. She only had to remember how her own mother had suffered to know that she would never risk making that mistake.

'Looks like someone's been busy,' Matt observed as he came into the room. Catherine saw him glance at her but she pretended not to notice as she screwed the cap back on her pen. Maybe she should feel relieved that she was back on track once more, but the fact that she'd needed to *remind* herself of the dangers of getting involved with him simply proved that she needed to be constantly on her guard.

'So what's the problem, Beck?' He glanced at the books spread across his desk. 'Are you stuck on your homework?'

'I was but Catherine has sorted it all out for me.' Becky grinned as she gathered up her homework. 'Thanks, Catherine. Your French is heaps better than Dad's. It's such a long time since he was at school that he's forgotten most of the things he learned!'

'Cheeky monkey!' Matt aimed a playful cuff at his daughter's ear. He glowered when Becky grinned and skipped out of the way. 'I'll remember that the next time you ask me for help, young lady.'

'I'll get Catherine to help me instead,' Becky retorted. 'She's brilliant at French!'

'Is she indeed?' Matt glanced at her and Catherine felt her pulse leap when she saw the warmth in his eyes. 'It looks as though I made the right decision by offering her a job here. She's not only a wonderful doctor but she's also great at doing homework. I wonder what other talents she's keeping hidden from us?'

Catherine had no idea what to say. Maybe it was her imagination but the air suddenly seemed to be charged with tension. It was a relief when a piping little voice suddenly butted in and spared her having to think up a reply.

'If Catherine has doned your homework, Becky, then can she read me a storwy now?'

She turned towards the door and saw Hannah standing there. The little girl smiled beseechingly as she showed Catherine the book she was holding. 'Will you, Catherine? Please?'

Catherine looked helplessly from the child to Matt, hoping he would help her out of her predicament, but he was trying hard not to laugh. 'I did warn you. I said that Hannah has a positive talent for coming up on your blind side!'

Catherine tried her best to think of an excuse but she simply couldn't find it in her heart to disappoint the little girl. 'Very well. But just one story, mind you!'

'Course,' Hannah agreed blithely. She took hold of Catherine's hand. 'Come on, Catherine. I'll show you where my bedroom is. We can snuggle up together under the quilt while you read to me.'

Catherine let herself be led from the room even though she could hear warning bells clanging inside her head. She knew it was a mistake to let herself get involved this way but she couldn't seem to stop what was happening. She sighed as she followed Hannah up the stairs. Working at Brookdale Surgery seemed to entail a lot more than simply doing her job.

'''And the two frogs stayed in the pond and lived happily ever after.'''

Catherine closed the book, wondering if Hannah really was asleep now. Each time she'd tried to make her escape the little girl had opened her eyes and begged her to read her another story. However, it appeared that she had finally dozed off.

She switched off the lamp and crept out of the room then nearly leapt out of her skin when she spotted Matt leaning against the landing wall.

'I was just coming to see how you were getting on,' he explained. 'I know what a little horror Hannah can be when she coerces someone into reading to her. She *never* lets them get away with just one story. How many did it take tonight?'

'Six, but at least she's asleep now and that's the main thing.'

She summoned a smile as she edged past him to get to the stairs. The bedrooms were on the top floor of the house and the landing was very narrow so there wasn't much room to pass. She bit her lip when her shoulder brushed Matt's chest and she suddenly discovered just how hard and warm his body felt beneath that thin cotton shirt.

'Well, I really appreciate it, Catherine. Thanks for being so patient with her.' He grimaced as he flattened himself against the wall. 'There's not much room up here, I'm afraid. Of course, this would have been the servants' quarters in the good old days. The family who originally owned this house wouldn't have ventured up this far so there was no need to make the landings any wider.'

'Oh, um…I hadn't realised that.' Catherine was having

great difficulty following the conversation. She quickly made her way down the stairs, hoping that he hadn't noticed her abstraction. Why had the feel of his body sent her mind into such a spin? she wondered. It certainly wasn't the first time that she'd been in such close contact with a man yet she couldn't remember ever feeling so aware of anyone before. It just seemed to prove what a mistake it would be to let herself get involved with him.

'You don't have to rush off, do you? I was hoping that you might stay and have supper with me.'

Matt laid a detaining hand on her arm and Catherine ground to a halt. He wasn't holding her tightly yet she could feel the separate imprint each of his fingers were making on her flesh. She had the craziest feeling that she would be able to see where his hand had been once he let her go, almost as though he had *branded* her with his touch.

She sucked in her breath, scarcely able to believe what was happening. She had to stop doing this! She had to start acting like herself and not like this person she seemed to be turning into. She opened her mouth to explain that she couldn't possibly stay when Matt forestalled her.

'Don't tell me you're washing your hair?'

'Pardon?' Her bewilderment was clear to see and he laughed.

'I got the distinct impression that you were hunting for an excuse to turn me down.' He shrugged but his gaze was searching all of a sudden. 'Hair-washing is the number-one pretext, I believe.'

'And is that based on personal experience?' Catherine was appalled when she realised what she'd said but he seemed unfazed by the question.

'No. But, then, I'm not really well versed in these matters. It's been a long time since I asked a woman to share my supper, or much else, for that matter. How about you, Catherine? Have you used that excuse very often to avoid hurting a would-be suitor's feelings?'

Oh, that was a tricky one! An affirmative would imply that she had men *queuing* up just to ask her for a date, whilst a negative would make it appear as though she rarely received an invitation. Catherine bit her lip in a quandary of indecision, which was so out of character that it just made the situation worse. It was a relief when Matt suddenly laughed.

'Sorry! I really shouldn't ask questions like that, should I? Let's start again and this time we won't let things get too complicated. If you don't have any plans for this evening, Catherine, would you like to stay for supper? It would save you having to cook a meal when you get home.'

Was that why he'd asked her in the first place? she wondered, trying to ignore a faint and totally irrational feeling of disappointment. He probably felt guilty because she'd stayed so late, reading to Hannah, and was trying to make up for it.

It was on the tip of her tongue to refuse when she suddenly thought better of it. It was almost eight o'clock and the thought of having to start cooking herself a meal at that time of the night wasn't very appealing.

'Then thank you, I'd like to stay. I'm absolutely starving and I really don't feel like cooking when I get in. I'll probably end up making myself a slice of toast and that'll be it.'

'Then you definitely must stay! A slice of toast indeed.' He shook his head as he led the way to the sitting room and opened the door. 'Go on in and make yourself comfortable while I open a bottle of wine. We can have a glass while we're waiting for the casserole to heat up.'

Catherine went into the room as he hurried away and took a long look around. It was the first time she'd been in this part of the house and she had to admit that she was curious. She wasn't sure what the room had been used as originally but the ornate plasterwork on the ceiling and the intricate parquet flooring suggested that it might have been the drawing room when the house had been built. Matt had turned it into a comfortable family living room and she had to admit that she liked what she saw.

The walls were papered in a rose pattern which perfectly suited the period of the house. Two huge velvet sofas placed either side of the fireplace provided a cosy seating area. There were a number of small tables dotted around the room, holding a variety of knick-knacks which the family must have collected over the years. Although everywhere was spotlessly clean, the furniture looked just a little shabby and the worse for wear, but that only seemed to add to the room's overall appeal. Catherine felt instantly at home as she sat down on one of the sofas, which was odd, really, because the decor in her own living room bore little resemblance to this.

'Right, here we go. I've opened a bottle of red—I hope that's all right. I seem to have run out of white.'

Matt came back with the wine and some glasses. He placed them on the coffee-table then unloaded a plate of cheese and crackers from the tray as well. 'I thought these would stave off your hunger while we're waiting for the casserole to heat up. I don't want you passing out. It wouldn't be good for my reputation if the patients found out that I worked my colleagues to the point of exhaustion!'

'That sounds very much like bribery to me. You'll feed me cheese and crackers so that I won't tell anyone how hard you make me work.'

'How did you guess?' Matt grinned as he offered her the plate. 'Let's hope it works.'

'You'll just have to wait and see, won't you?' she retorted, popping a cube of cheese into her mouth. She quickly ate it then smiled at him. 'I just love this room, Matt. It's really cosy in here.'

'Thank you, although I can't really claim any credit for it. I'm the world's worst when it comes to choosing colours and things. That was Ruth's department so she's the one who chose the colour scheme in here.'

He filled their glasses and sat down. 'I haven't redecorated the room since she died so it's still very much how she wanted it to look. I've just added a few bits and pieces, here and there.'

'Well, it looks lovely, whoever chose the decor,' she said firmly, wondering why the mention of his wife should have caused her such a pang.

'I'm glad you like it. I just wanted it to be somewhere the kids could do their homework and watch TV or whatever. It didn't seem important if everything was perfectly co-ordinated.'

'That's probably why it works so well. It looks as though the room has *evolved*.'

'That's a good way to describe it!' He laughed as he picked up a cracker. 'There certainly hasn't been a lot of thought gone into it in recent years. Bits and bobs have been added as and when the girls and I have found them.'

'What do you mean by you *found* them?' Catherine asked curiously.

'If I let you into a secret, will you swear not to reveal it to anyone?'

She stared at him in astonishment. 'Well, yes, I suppose so.'

'We're car boot sale fanatics. There is nothing the three of us like better than taking off on a Sunday morning and having a good old rummage around in other people's cast-offs.'

'Really?'

'Yes, really.' He picked up a small silver dish from the coffee-table and gave it to her. 'We found this a couple a weeks ago. It was all black and tarnished when Becky spotted it but see how beautifully it's cleaned up.'

Catherine couldn't hide her amazement. 'But it's exquisite!'

'It is. I imagine it must be worth quite a bit of money

and definitely more than the fifty pence Becky paid for it. However, that isn't the reason we go hunting for treasure.'

Matt's smile was reflective as he took the bowl from her. 'It's just a great way for us to enjoy a morning out together. We're out in the fresh air—even if it does usually rain—plus there is the thrill of wondering if you're going to find something exciting. It also helps the girls to realise that you don't have to spend a fortune to have fun. When you're a single parent there is always a danger that you try to overcompensate by buying things for the children. But money isn't the be-all and end-all, is it?'

'No, I suppose it isn't,' Catherine said slowly.

Her heart leapt because if Matt had asked her that a few days ago, she would have found it impossible to agree with him. There had never been any money to spare while she'd been growing up and she had often resented it. It was one of the reasons why she had always been so determined to make a success of her life, but Matt's comment suddenly made her wonder if money really was the answer to every problem. Was she making a mistake by concentrating on achieving material gain rather than personal happiness?

It was impossible to answer that question with any degree of certainty but she couldn't deny that she'd been touched by what he'd told her. It just proved how much thought and effort he put into raising his children. How long had he been doing it on his own? she wondered, and knew she had to find out.

'How long is it since your wife died, Matt?'

'Five years—just a month before Hannah's first birthday, in fact.' He put the bowl back on the table and sighed. 'Ruth found out that she had ovarian cancer at the same time that she found out she was pregnant with Hannah. She refused to have treatment because it would have meant her having a termination and that just wasn't an option for her.'

'Oh, how awful! How did you feel—about her refusing treatment, I mean?' Catherine couldn't begin to imagine how hard it must have been for him to deal with his wife's decision.

'I think I ran the whole gamut of emotions, to tell the truth. I wanted Ruth to have treatment yet I knew it would be wrong to try and force her to do something she was totally opposed to. Ruth had a very strong faith and termination—for any reason—wasn't an option for her.'

He smiled but his eyes were sad. 'I suppose I kept hoping that once the baby was born, something could be done for Ruth, but it was too late by then. My only consolation is that Ruth was so happy when Hannah was born safe and sound.'

'I'm sorry.' It sounded so trite yet Catherine really meant it.

'So am I. But Ruth wouldn't have wanted me to spend my life grieving for her because she wasn't that sort of person. I have the children to consider as well. Looking after them has been my number-one priority these past few years.'

'And you've never thought about getting married again?' She hadn't meant to ask such a personal question but he didn't appear to mind.

'No.' He shrugged but there was something in his eyes which made her heart start to race all of a sudden. 'I've never found anyone I wanted to marry until now. Right, that casserole should be just about ready. I'll go and see.'

He got up and left the room. Catherine picked up her glass and drank some of the wine although she had no idea how it tasted. All she could think about was what Matt had said. He'd not thought about remarrying because he'd never met anyone he wanted to marry—*until now*.

She put the glass down with a small thud. Surely he hadn't been referring to her?

CHAPTER FIVE

'THAT was delicious.'

Catherine leant back in her seat with a sigh of contentment. 'Your mother really is the most wonderful cook.'

'Isn't she just?' Matt finished his last mouthful of casserole and put down his fork. 'Mind you, she's had years of practice. She and my father ran their own catering company until he died. Mum oversaw all the menus and woe betide the chefs if the food wasn't up to her exacting standards.'

'I can imagine!' Catherine smiled. She'd done her best not to think about what Matt had said while they'd been eating but it hadn't been easy. The idea that he might be harbouring such feelings about her made her feel very mixed up. Although she knew that she must make it clear that there was no chance of them having a relationship, she couldn't deny that she was more than merely flattered by the idea.

She pushed the thought to the back of her mind because it was too difficult to deal with it at that moment. 'Why did she give up the business? Was it too much for her to manage on her own?'

'That's what she claims although I'm not sure if I believe her.' His tone was sombre all of a sudden. 'Mum would never admit it but I think the deciding factor was because she wanted to help me look after the girls. I doubt I could have managed without her help when they were younger either.'

'Did you never consider getting a nanny?'

'I did, but Mum talked me out of it. She said it would be better for Becky and Hannah to have someone they

71

knew looking after them, someone who would be there on a permanent basis. I realised that she was right so accepted her offer to come and live with us.'

His tone implied that he still felt guilty about it and she hurried to reassure him. 'Maybe looking after the children helps her as much as it does you.'

She saw him frown and hurried on, suddenly wishing that she'd kept her opinions to herself. It really wasn't wise to involve herself in his affairs, but it was hard to remain impartial when he seemed so intent on blaming himself.

'It must have been a shock for her when your father died. Helping you look after the children probably helped your mother get over it by giving her something positive to focus on.'

'You're right, of course. I should have realised that myself.' Matt's smile was warm as he reached over the table and squeezed her hand. 'Thanks, Catherine. I have to confess that it's always worried me that Mum gave up so much because of me. Now I can see that it probably helped her come to terms with my father's death. They had a wonderful marriage and I know how much she misses him even now.'

'I...I'm sure you would have realised it sooner or later.' It was difficult to form a coherent sentence when she was so conscious of him touching her. Catherine tried to ease her hand free but he held onto it.

'Maybe, but it still helped to have you point it out.' He gave her fingers another gentle squeeze then let her go. Contrarily, Catherine immediately wished that he hadn't released her because it felt as though she had been suddenly cast adrift.

Maybe it was a ridiculous notion but she couldn't ignore it. Hadn't she already admitted that she found Matt's dependability one of his most attractive features? There was a steadiness about him, a rock-like firmness which was extremely appealing. He would be the perfect anchor in a time of crisis, she thought with a little leap of her heart, a man who would never let you down.

'I suppose I've been too busy to really think about it before. Just getting through an average day seems to be a Herculean task!'

'It must be difficult.' She fixed a smile into place when he carried on speaking, praying that he couldn't tell how on edge she felt. She mustn't fall into the trap of letting herself depend on Matt, or any other man for that matter. It would be a mistake. 'Juggling a career and a family can't be easy for anyone.'

'It isn't, although it's what an awful lot of women do. They manage to do a full-time job and still be a mother and a homemaker.' He shook his head. 'They say that men aren't as good as women are at keeping all the balls in the air at once, and I for one wouldn't dispute that. What about you, Catherine? Will you carry on working after you have a family?'

'I hadn't really thought about it,' she replied, uncomfortable with the direction the conversation was going. She couldn't explain it but she knew how shocked Matt would be if she told him that she had decided never to have any children.

'No? Funny, I imagined that you would have had it all worked out. You seem to know exactly what you want from life from what I've seen.'

He was right, of course, because she'd always known what she wanted. Or so she had believed until recently.

Catherine hastily stood up, not wanting to expand on that thought. So maybe she *had* been behaving rather strangely since she'd come to Brookdale Surgery but it didn't mean that her future plans had altered. She knew *exactly* what she was going to do with her life and that hadn't changed.

'And right now I think it's about time I went home.' She deftly turned the remark into a joke, smiling when

Matt stood up as well. 'Thanks for the meal. I really enjoyed it.'

'And thank you for the company. That was the best part of all.'

His tone was light and she breathed a sigh of relief. It made her earlier fears seem rather foolish, in fact. They were just two colleagues who'd spent some time together after work. There was nothing at all to suggest that Matt hoped they would become more than that. If he *had* met someone whom he was hoping would become a major part of his life, it certainly wasn't her.

The realisation was rather deflating for some reason. Catherine determinedly put it out of her head while Matt saw her out. He insisted on accompanying her downstairs and waiting while she fetched her coat from the staffroom even though she assured him she could manage.

'Allow me.'

He took the coat from her and held it out with a flourish so that she could slip her arms into the sleeves. Catherine shivered when she felt his fingers brushing her neck as he smoothed the collar into place. She moved away, drawing the warm, grey flannel around her as she tried to ignore the little ripples of awareness that were spreading across her neck.

'Thank you again for the meal and everything,' she said stiffly.

'And thank you again for the company and everything.'

He gently mocked her formality and she felt her cheeks redden. Hurrying to the door, she reached for the handle only to find that Matt had got to it first. Their hands collided and she heard the swift, indrawn breath he took...

Her eyes rose to his as though drawn by some force beyond her control and she saw the tenderness they held as his head lowered. His lips brushed her cheek and she shivered when she felt a wave of sensation wash through her. He drew the coat collar up around her neck as he stepped back and his eyes were filled with warmth.

'I'll see you tomorrow, Catherine. Drive carefully.'

Catherine nodded purely and simply because she didn't know what to say. Maybe she should have told him that he shouldn't have kissed her, that it was inappropriate for him to behave that way, but she was afraid that the words wouldn't come out the way she wanted them to.

She quickly left the surgery and hurried to her car. Matt was still standing at the door and he waved as she drove past. Catherine desperately wanted to wave back just to prove that she was in control, only her hands refused to obey her. She let herself into her flat a short time later, overwhelmed by relief that she was home. At least here she knew who she was. She was safe here in the world she had created for herself.

She took off her coat then went into the sitting room and stood there for a moment, waiting for the usual feeling of peace to envelop her. Usually, coming home to her own private space was soothing after a busy day at work but tonight the feeling of calm evaded her. The room looked as it always did—peaceful, perfect, orderly—but it was impossible to draw any comfort from her surroundings when her thoughts were in such turmoil.

She closed her eyes and Matt was suddenly there inside her head—his smile, his warmth, the hardness of his body, the gentle, *tender* feel of his mouth as it had touched her cheek. A single tear spilled from her eyes and trickled down her cheek. That was all she could allow herself, just one tear. It was too dangerous to give in to all the emotions churning inside her, too risky; it went against every rule she lived by. A single tear was all she could spare yet it felt as though every bit of emotion she had kept pent up inside her was contained in that drop as it slid down her cheek…the cheek which Matt had kissed.

'Hello, Mr Marshall, I'm Catherine Lewis. I believe Dr Fielding phoned to let you know that I'd be coming to see you this afternoon.'

It was Thursday afternoon and it should have been her afternoon off but, mindful of her promise to Matt, Catherine had gone to visit David Marshall, the patient with motor neurone disease. She had been surprised by how big the house was when she had turned into the drive. Matt had given her directions on how to find it but he had failed to mention how enormous the property was. With its walled gardens and terraces, the house had to be worth a fortune by London standards. It had made her wonder what sort of reception she would receive from the owner but she needn't have worried. David Marshall looked absolutely delighted to see her.

'So he did. He said I'd be in for a treat and he was right, too. There's nothing like having a beautiful young woman dancing attendance on you to cheer a guy up!'

Catherine laughed. 'Thank you...I think!'

She followed him into the study, covertly studying him as she sat down. She knew from his records that David was in his early fifties although he looked much older because of the devastating effects of the disease. He must have been a powerfully built man at one time, but the characteristic muscle wastage caused by his illness had left him looking extremely gaunt and haggard. Nevertheless, there was a definite twinkle in his eyes as he positioned his wheelchair so they were facing one another. 'So what's your opinion? How long do you think I have left on this mortal coil? Or are you the sort of doctor who doesn't believe in telling a patient the truth?'

She laughed. 'It all depends on the patient.'

'I see. Well, I promise you that I won't go to pieces, Catherine...I hope you don't mind me calling you that but it seems pointless standing on ceremony, doesn't it?' He gave a deep laugh. 'One of the joys of being an invalid is that people rarely take offence when you overstep the normal social boundaries.'

'I don't mind at all so long as I can call you David,'

she replied lightly. 'And I admire the fact that you can find something positive about your illness.'

'It's more a question of necessity than choice. I've long since come to terms with the fact that I either accept what is happening to me or spend my remaining days feeling bitter. To my mind, that would be extremely pointless.'

Catherine nodded. 'I agree, although it's easy for me to say that when I'm not the one who's ill.'

'Oh, I imagine you'd feel much the same if it was you sitting in this chair.' David studied her thoughtfully. 'There's a great deal of strength in your face, Catherine, and determination, too. You're a fighter. I can tell that just by looking at you.'

She laughed although the comment had disconcerted her. It wasn't usual for people to pass remarks like that. She had always taken care to distance herself and never encouraged the kind of relationship that allowed for personal comments. It made her wonder what had changed. Had she become more open since she'd met Matt, perhaps?

Her heart lurched when she realised how much of an effect he was having on her life. She'd spoken to him only briefly that morning and then only because she'd been unable to avoid it. She'd spent a restless night going over everything that had happened yet by the time dawn had broken she still hadn't been able to rationalise her feelings. There was something about Matt which made it very difficult to put him into any kind of a category, which was her usual way of dealing with people. Matt was Matt, and it wasn't easy to judge him against all the usual stereotypes.

She suddenly became aware of the silence and realised that David was waiting for her to reply. 'You're right. I *am* a pretty determined person once I set my mind to it.'

'I thought so. I've become quite an observer of people since I've been confined to this contraption. I've become a watcher rather than a doer and have discovered talents I didn't know I had!'

He laughed but Catherine heard the regret in his voice. She knew better than to sympathise with him, however, so smoothly changed the subject. 'Matt told me that you used to play rugby for England.'

'That's right.'

David sounded much more cheerful as he began regaling her with tales of his exploits when he'd been a member of the England squad. He was an amusing raconteur and she enjoyed hearing what he'd got up to although she couldn't help noticing that he was becoming breathless as he spoke. As the disease progressed, the muscles involved in breathing and swallowing became affected and it was the deterioration of these muscles which usually led to a person's death. She found herself thinking how sad it was that such a vital man should have been so cruelly struck down.

'It sounds as though you had a lot of fun,' she declared when David came to the end of his tale. She opened her case to find her sphygmomanometer so she could to take his blood pressure. Matt had impressed on her how important it was to justify her visit and she intended to follow his advice.

'I did. I packed a lot of living into those years, I can tell you.' David treated her to a wry smile. 'Do we really have to go through this charade? I'd much rather we just sat and talked.'

'Charade?' Catherine repeated uncertainly, then caught sight of his face. She shook her head as she closed her case. 'How long have you suspected that it was just a ruse?'

'Oh, ages. I just didn't want to disappoint Matt.' David's tone was wry. 'He's a great guy and I know that he thinks he's fooling me by doing all these checks, but I'm well aware that he and Glenda come here to keep my spirits up. For me that's the best medicine in the world so I certainly wasn't going to let on that I'd sussed him out!'

'I see. So how come you've owned up to me?' Catherine asked with a laugh.

'I suppose it's because I'm tired of pretending. If I've only got a short time left then it's a shame to waste it. I don't want sympathy, but I do appreciate the fact that there are people kind enough to come here and cheer me up.' David looked her straight in the eyes. 'So no more charades, Catherine. At least not for you and me. As for Matt...well, I'd hate to hurt his feelings.'

'So you'll keep on letting him take your blood pressure and whatever else he can come up with?' Catherine pulled a face. 'I don't know if I should be aiding and abetting you in deceiving a colleague.'

'There's no harm in it. Anyway, tell me what you've been up to since you started working at the surgery. There's nothing I like better than hearing what's going on in the world beyond these four walls.'

Surprisingly, the next hour flew past. David was easy to talk to and had a very astute mind. She found herself telling him about Mrs Grimes's predicament, and how the phone call she'd made that morning to the housing department had achieved very little result.

David frowned as he weighed up what he'd heard. 'So the poor old soul is in danger of being parted from the only thing she cares about, her cat? That seems very callous to me.'

'Doesn't it? I know it must be difficult to find the right accommodation for everyone but it seems so heartless to take away the one thing the old lady loves. And if you saw where she's living at the moment!' Catherine shuddered.

'It makes me realise how lucky I am,' David observed. 'I have this huge house and people to look after me. It's a waste in a way because I have nobody to leave it to when I die. Maybe it would make sense to turn this place into a home where people like that old lady could live out their remaining years in peace. It's usually lack of money which puts people in that kind of a situation, isn't it?'

'It is.' Catherine glanced at her watch and stood up. 'It's

time I was going. It's been a pleasure meeting you, David. I've really enjoyed our talk.'

'So have I.' David smiled at her. 'I hope you'll come again soon and that you won't let on to Matt that I've sussed him out.'

'Cross my heart and hope to die!' she promised, making a cross over her heart.

'Good. It will be our secret.' David followed her out of the room. His wheelchair was state of the art, needing minimal effort to make it run smoothly. He stopped beside the front door and his tone was a shade too casual to be convincing. 'By the way, how's Ann these days?'

'Ann Talbot, do you mean?' Catherine asked, wanting to be sure he was referring to their practice nurse.

'That's right. I haven't seen her in a while and I was just wondering how she was.'

'She's fine,' Catherine assured him, wondering if it had been just a polite enquiry. Had David and Ann had a more *personal* relationship than that of patient and nurse, perhaps?

'I'll tell her that you were asking after her, shall I?' she offered.

'If you like.'

The dismissive note in David's voice didn't quite ring true.

Catherine sighed as got into her car. It looked as though another relationship had hit the rocks. It made her see how wise she'd been to steer clear of any romantic involvement. Once love entered the equation, common sense flew out of the window, as her mother had been so fond of saying.

She frowned because all of a sudden the words didn't seem to carry as much weight as they had once done. How strange.

'So how was David yesterday when you saw him?'

Catherine looked up from the notes she'd been writing

when Matt tapped on her door. It was a few minutes before surgery started on Friday morning. She'd got in early that day, hoping to catch up with the backlog of paperwork that had accumulated during the week. Most days she was too busy to do more than make the briefest notes after she had seen a patient and there were a number of cases that required a more detailed report. So far she'd managed to complete just half a dozen but it was a start.

'Not too bad. He was a bit breathless but that's only to be expected at this stage,' she replied evenly, even though her heart had seemed to fit in an extra beat when Matt had appeared.

'Good. I'm keeping my fingers crossed that he doesn't deteriorate too rapidly over the next few months.' He sighed. 'I know it's impossible to foretell how quickly the disease will progress, but the fact that David was so fit initially should work in his favour. He's also very good about sticking to his physiotherapy regime and I'm sure that helps.'

'He seems to have a very positive view although it can't have been easy for him, coming to terms with his illness,' she observed, wondering why the sight of Matt should have this effect on her. It wasn't as though he was spectacularly handsome although his craggily attractive features would appeal to many women. She sighed because whenever she tried to rationalise her response to him she ended up feeling more confused.

'It wasn't, especially when his wife decided that she couldn't handle the thought of him becoming dependent on her.'

Matt's expression was sombre as he came into the room. 'David reached an all-time low after she left him. I was really worried that he would give up. However, he seemed to rally, mainly thanks to Ann. She managed to talk some sense into him.'

'He mentioned Ann, funnily enough.' Catherine

frowned as she thought back to the conversation she'd had with David about their practice nurse.

'And?' Matt prompted.

'And I wondered if something had gone on between them, something more than Ann just being his nurse.'

'I've wondered about that, too. However, when I tried broaching the subject, David clammed up.' He shrugged. 'I didn't like to ask Ann because she's such a private person.'

Catherine frowned. Matt didn't seem to have any qualms about asking *her* personal questions and it made her wonder how he viewed her. Most people were put off by the cool aura she projected but it didn't seem to bother him. Maybe he sensed that it was just a front?

It was unsettling to wonder if he was astute enough to see past the barriers with which she surrounded herself so it was a relief when he changed the subject.

'I got onto Social Services about Mrs Grimes, by the way, but they weren't much help. Their view is that the council is responsible for rehousing her and it isn't their problem. Apparently, the council wants all the flats cleared before Christmas because building work is due to start at the beginning of January. They've sold them to a private developer and there's a penalty clause in the contract that comes into force if all the tenants haven't been moved out by then. The council stands to lose thousands of pounds so that's why they're taking such a tough stand.'

'But it's only a month till Christmas!' Catherine exclaimed in dismay. 'I'm sure Mrs Grimes doesn't know that she's going to be put out of her flat so soon because she hasn't mentioned it. It will break her heart if she has to part with her cat, especially at Christmas-time. Surely there must be someone who can do something to help?'

'Age Concern might be able to give us some advice. I could try them.'

'Would you? We have to do something, Matt. That cat is the only thing she lives for!'

'Then I'll see what they suggest.' His smile was strangely gentle and she frowned.

'What's that funny look for?'

'Oh, nothing, really. It's just that you give the impression that nothing ever touches you, but you're not at all like that, are you, Catherine? You really do care about people you treat despite that cool face you present to the world.'

'I just don't like to see people taken advantage of,' she snapped, hating the fact that the comment had made her feel so vulnerable. 'It's not a question of whether or not I care, but a simple matter of justice!'

'Of course. Sorry. I obviously misunderstood.' His tone gently mocked her and she felt a wash of colour run up her face when she realised that she hadn't fooled him. She did care, and she cared a great deal, but she preferred to keep her emotions safely locked away rather than wear her heart on her sleeve.

She picked up her pen, hoping Matt would take the hint and leave. Little by little he seemed to whittling away at her composure, making her expose a bit more of herself each time. It scared her because she wasn't sure what would happen if he managed to peel away all her defensive layers.

'I'd better get to work.' He grimaced as he headed for the door. 'I need to pull out all the stops today. It's parents' night at Becky's school this evening and I don't want to run over time for a change.'

He paused by the door. 'Talking about school just reminded me that there's a Christmas fair there on Saturday afternoon. How would you fancy coming with us? They're having a car boot sale as well so you never know what treasures you might unearth.'

Catherine shook her head. 'It's kind of you to invite me but I've already made plans. Friends of mine have just moved into a new flat and they've invited me for lunch.'

'I see. I expect it will be a bit more sophisticated than

rooting around in other people's rubbish.' He laughed but she saw the disappointment in his blue eyes. 'Not to worry. Maybe another time.'

He left the room and Catherine bit her lip. She had the most insane desire to call him back and tell him that she had changed her mind. She sighed because it would be a mistake to do that. She couldn't afford to get involved in his life but it was so difficult to remain detached. Maybe it would help if she reminded herself of what she really wanted from life.

Picking up her pen, she wrote it all down on the blotter. Number one on the list was to use her time here at Brookdale Surgery to further her experience. Number two was to find suitable premises for her own practice. Number three had to be to make her practice just as successful as possible. Number four...

She stopped because she had no idea what number four should be. She had never gone past the point of forging a successful career before so couldn't imagine what else she wanted from life. Of course, most women wanted to find someone to love and have a family with, but that was out of the question for her. Love and marriage simply didn't go hand in hand with a successful career and she had no intention of compromising.

Catherine screwed the paper into a ball and tossed it into the waste bin. There was an ache in her heart all of a sudden but she refused to think about the reason for it. She had made her plans and nothing and nobody was going to sway her from the course she'd chosen. She was going to make a success of her life, she really was. She didn't need love or a family to be happy.

Did she?

CHAPTER SIX

'So I told them that I wouldn't take their wretched job if they paid me double the salary!'

Catherine smiled politely as the man beside her came to the end of a long and exceedingly boring tale. The lunch party was in full flow and everyone, apart from her, seemed to be enjoying themselves immensely. Her friends, Patricia and Max, had spent a fortune having their new flat decorated to their exacting standards. Catherine had made all the right noises when she'd been shown around but she had found herself comparing the tasteful decor to the cosy, lived-in atmosphere Matt had created in his home. She knew in her heart which she preferred.

Impatient with herself for letting thoughts of Matt intrude yet again, she tried to concentrate as the man beside her began yet another long-winded tale of his triumphs. However, her heart really wasn't in the conversation so that when someone mentioned Peter Hoskins's name she was immediately distracted. She couldn't help wondering if it was the same Peter Hoskins she'd heard of only that week—the husband of her mystery patient, Lauren.

Catherine frowned as she caught the tail end of the conversation, something about Peter Hoskins having lost his job. She would have dearly loved to verify if it was indeed the same person but it was impossible with the man beside her monopolising her attention. It was a relief when Patricia announced that coffee would be served in the drawing room because it meant that she could make her escape.

'It's been absolutely lovely, Patricia, but I'll have to skip coffee, I'm afraid,' she explained as everyone got up. 'There's a few things I need to sort out.'

'Oh, who'd be a doctor?' Patricia trilled. 'Never a moment to oneself!'

Catherine smiled because it was easier to let the woman think what she chose. Although she had known Patricia and Max for a number of years, they weren't really close friends. She had a sneaking suspicion that they used her to make up the numbers, which could explain why she had been seated next to Mr Boring today.

She said her goodbyes, politely cutting short her table companion's attempts to get her phone number. She certainly didn't want to have to sit through another hour of his monologues! It was a relief to be outside at last even though the weather had taken a decided turn for the worse. There was a bitterly cold wind blowing along the street as she started walking home and the threat of rain in the sky. However, Catherine didn't hurry as she headed back to her flat. There was nobody waiting for her to get back and nothing to hurry for. The thought was oddly depressing.

'Catherine! Over here!'

She stopped when she heard someone calling her name and felt her heart lift when she saw Matt leaning out of his car window. She waited for a gap in the traffic then ran across the road to speak to him.

'Hello! What are you doing here?' she demanded, crouching down so that she could see through the window.

'We're going to the Christmas fair!' Hannah announced from the back seat before Matt could answer. 'Tell her, Daddy!'

'Yes, ma'am!' Matt replied, saluting smartly as he got out of the car. He took hold of Catherine's arm and quickly steered her onto the pavement out of the way of the traffic. 'I mentioned it to you the other day, if you remember.'

'I do,' Catherine agreed, thinking how good he looked that day. The well-worn jeans clung to his long legs, emphasising his muscular thighs, whilst the heavy, navy sweater he wore with them made his shoulders look broader than ever. Her heart seemed to skip a beat when she realised just how attractive he looked. She fixed a determined smile to her mouth although it wavered a little when she realised Matt was subjecting her to an equally thorough scrutiny.

Did he think the plum-coloured sweater she was wearing with her new grey wool trouser suit suited her? she wondered. And did he like the way she'd done her hair that day, twisting it into a knot on the crown of her head, a style which showed off her slender neck and delicate ears?

Yes and yes again, a voice inside her declared triumphantly. He liked everything he saw!

Catherine quickly cleared her throat and heard Matt clear his as well. For some reason that seemed to make her vocal cords tie themselves in knots all over again so that she had to do it a second time but so, too, did he. The situation was in serious danger of turning into a farce, she thought, her heart hammering wildly inside her chest. It was a relief when Becky unwittingly saved the day.

'Why don't you come with us to the fair, Catherine? There'll be loads of things to buy. My class is selling Christmas cards and wrapping paper so you could buy some there to save you having to go to the shops.'

'Oh, I don't know,' she demurred, not sure it would be wise to put herself under any more pressure. There was no point pretending that Matt didn't have the strangest effect on her so surely it would be more sensible to limit the amount of time they spent together?

'That's a good idea! Do say you'll come, Cathy.' Matt turned to the children. 'We'd love to have Catherine come with us, wouldn't we, kids?'

It was hard to refuse when Hannah and Becky added their pleas to his. Catherine held out for a few seconds longer but it was almost a foregone conclusion that she would have to give in eventually. Was that why Matt had enlisted the children's help? she wondered as she slid into the front seat of the car after Becky quickly vacated it. Because he knew how difficult it would be to refuse them?

'It's amazing how hard it is to refuse a child, isn't it, Cathy?'

Matt's voice was low enough not to carry to where the children were sitting in the back. Catherine looked at him in surprise and had to laugh when she saw the wicked smile he gave her.

'You conniving wretch, Matt Fielding! There should be a name for people like you who use their children to their own ends.'

'Oh, I'm sure there is. Still, all's fair in love and war, as they say.'

He treated her to another dazzling smile as he started the engine. Catherine took a deep breath. She wasn't even going to *try* to work out what he'd meant by that!

'Do you really *need* another teddy bear, Hannah?'

Matt's tone rippled with exasperation and Catherine tried hard not to laugh. They were standing in the middle of the school hall where a selection of stalls had been set up. As it was so close to Christmas, the children had decorated the hall with yards of shiny tinsel and everywhere looked very festive. There was a huge variety of goods on sale, ranging from home-made cakes to second-hand toys. Hannah had made a beeline for the toy stall as soon as they'd arrived and had managed to buy no less than three ragged teddy bears in the short time they'd been there.

'Yes,' Hannah stated emphatically. 'My teddies need lots of new friends to play with. Please, can I buy him, Daddy? Please!'

'OK, you win. How much is he?' Matt counted out the requisite 50 p. He shook his head as the little girl went racing off to make her purchase. 'We have a cupboard at home absolutely stuffed to bursting with teddy bears. Hannah seems to believe it's her mission in life to rescue every rejected bear, no matter what deplorable state it's in.'

'It just proves what a kind heart she has,' Catherine stated with a sad lack of sympathy for his plight. 'I mean, would you really prefer to watch that poor old ted being carted off to the rubbish dump when you've got a nice warm cupboard going spare?'

'Prefer it? I'd drive the wretched bear there myself!'

His tone was so wry that she laughed. Matt pulled a face. 'Anyway, never mind trying to make me feel guilty. You tell me how you would feel about having to set to and perform major surgery after a full day at work.'

'Major surgery. What do you mean?' Catherine frowned and heard him chuckle.

'A lot of these rehomed teddies need surgery to patch up their wounds and that task falls to me. Then, of course, there are the ones who just need a bandage on their arms or legs, and some who only have a headache.' He rolled his eyes. 'I have almost as many teddy-bear patients at home as I have *real* ones in the surgery!'

Catherine couldn't stop laughing. Tears streamed from her eyes as she pressed a hand to her mouth to stifle her mirth. 'Don't! The thought of you playing doctor to a row of stuffed toys doesn't *bear* thinking about!'

Matt glowered at her pun. 'I don't know if I take kindly to being mocked like this, Dr Lewis. Have you forgotten your Hippocratic oath? You swore to do your best for *all* your patients, and as far as I recall there was no mention of the fact that those patients couldn't be *bears*.'

'I'm sure there wasn't.' Catherine mopped her streaming eyes and grinned at him. 'I honestly and truly can't recall there ever being an exclusion put on teddy bears!'

'Then I rest my case. Now, seeing as you saw fit to mock me, you deserve to be suitably punished.' Matt took her arm and steered her towards the door. 'Out into the cold for you, my girl. It's time we went to check out the car boot sale and see what treasures we can find, rather than lurking in here while we keep warm.'

'Oh, no! Not the cold-weather punishment. I don't think I can stand it,' Catherine declared, pulling up the collar of her jacket as they exited the school hall. She couldn't help thinking how unlike her it was to join in the fun like this. Usually she wouldn't have dreamt of going along with such nonsense but it was hard to stand on her dignity with Matt. He had a positive talent for making *any* situation seem acceptable.

Maybe the thought should have worried her but she was enjoying herself too much to want to put a stop to what was happening. She let Matt lead her outside to where quite a large number of cars had been parked in the playground. Catherine was surprised by how many people had turned up for the sale, and by how clued-up they all seemed to be as she listened to them haggling over prices. She mentioned it to Matt, who grinned.

'You aint seen nothing yet, kid! I pride myself on being a good haggler. Come on, let's see if I can put my talents to good use and buy you something.'

Before Catherine could protest that she didn't want him to buy her anything, he'd headed over to one of the cars and started searching through the goods on offer. She hung back, feeling a little awkward at first. However, she soon got into the swing of things and began poking around in the motley assortment of items for sale.

'How about this?' she asked, pulling a small trinket box out of a basket of odds and ends. The box was covered in seashells arranged in a concentric pattern and it really appealed to her even though several of the shells were missing.

'Mmm, let's have a look.' Matt took the box from her and opened the lid. 'Looks as though the missing shells are all in here so it shouldn't be difficult to repair it,' he advised her *sotto voce*.

Catherine took it from him. 'It's pretty, or it could be if it was cleaned up. How much do you think it costs?'

'Let's find out.' He waved to stall holder and asked the price, shaking his head when the woman named a sum he obviously considered too expensive. He halved it then added on a few pence when the seller refused *his* offer.

Catherine bit her lip as she listened to him haggling. For some reason it seemed really important that she got the box. She was actually holding her breath as she listened to Matt haggling over the price because she didn't want to lose it.

She needn't have worried. A few minutes later the box was hers and both Matt and the stall holder looked extremely satisfied with the sale. Catherine shook her head in amazement. 'I would never have had the nerve to haggle like that. How do you do it?'

'Having a thick skin helps,' he declared, looping a casual arm around her shoulders as he led her away from the car. 'But it's really a question of being an ace negotiator, of course.'

'Oh, of course!' She was achingly conscious of the weight of his arm on her shoulders yet it wasn't an unpleasant feeling—far from it. There was something deeply reassuring about feeling Matt's arm there as he steered her through the crowd, as though they could achieve anything if they stood shoulder to shoulder against the world.

She shivered when it struck her how stupid that thought was. The only person she could rely on was herself and she mustn't forget that. She would never put herself in the position her mother had been in and allow any man to let *her* down.

'Hey, you're shivering. Let's get back inside before you catch a chill.' Matt didn't wait for her to reply as he hurried her back inside the hall. He closed the door then rubbed his hands together. 'It's really freezing out there. How about a cup of coffee to warm us up?'

'Sounds good to me,' she agreed, trying to shake off the

feeling of sadness which had filled her. Maybe it appeared that some relationships would last for ever but she'd seen the statistics and knew just how many foundered. She'd also witnessed at first hand the devastation it caused when a marriage broke down and had sworn that she would never put herself through that kind of torment. She had been right to make the decision not to get romantically involved with anyone and it would be wrong to change her mind no matter how tempted she was.

'What about the children? Will they want a drink?' she asked, quickly changing the subject. She looked at the crowds milling around and frowned in concern. 'Where's Hannah? I can't see her anywhere.'

'Don't worry, she'll be fine,' Matt assured her. 'Before we go out anywhere the children and I make a contingency plan.'

'A contingency plan?'

'Yes. The thing I wanted to avoid was becoming an overly anxious parent. It isn't easy because something happens to you when you have children and your ability to spot danger at every turn seems to multiply a hundredfold.' His tone was light but Catherine sensed that it hadn't been easy for him to deal with his fears about the children's safety.

'I imagine it's hard to give children enough freedom and yet make sure that they're safe,' she suggested.

'Exactly. I don't want the girls growing up terrified of the world we live in. They have to be allowed to do things on their own—within certain limits, of course. That's why whenever we come to an event like this we make a plan so they know what they are allowed to do.'

'So what was today's plan?' Catherine asked, trying to match her tone to his even though it had touched her deeply to realise again how much thought he put into raising his daughters.

'That neither of them must leave the school grounds under any circumstances. Obviously, Becky, being that bit older, has a bit more freedom than Hannah, but she still has to follow the rules. As for Hannah, well, I've drummed it into her that she must stay with me or Becky at all times. She's probably helping Becky on the Christmas-card stall so let's go and find them.'

They made their way across the hall and, as Matt had predicted, the children were both busily working on the stall. Becky was taking the money while Hannah was wrapping up the cards after they were purchased. Both girls looked delighted to see them.

'Hi! What have you bought?' Becky demanded, relinquishing her place behind the counter to one of her classmates.

'This.' Catherine held up the trinket box for her inspection, smiling when Becky gave an appreciative whistle.

'Cool! I bet that cleans up really well. What do you think, Dad?'

'I think you're right. Actually, that box was probably made around the same time our house was built. Shell work was very popular in Victorian times,' he explained.

'Was it?' Catherine studied the box. 'I hadn't realised it was so old. Maybe you should have it for the sitting room. It would fit perfectly in there.'

She offered him the box but Matt shook his head. 'No way! It's your first bit of treasure trove so you must keep it as a talisman.'

'A talisman?'

'To bring you good luck the next time you come treasure-hunting with us, of course.'

He seemed to think it was a forgone conclusion that she'd go with them again and it seemed wrong to make a fuss in front of the children. She let it pass but made up her mind that she would make sure he understood it had been a one-off event as soon as she got the chance.

'Right, so who's for tea and cakes?' he asked.

'Me!' Hannah shouted, jumping up and down. She caught hold of Catherine's hand and towed her towards the tea stall, which was doing a roaring trade that day. 'Come on, Catherine. You, me and the teddies will find a table.'

Catherine let herself be led away, leaving it to Becky and Matt to fetch the tea. They were in luck because there was a couple just leaving and she and Hannah managed to get their table.

'Busy today, isn't it?' the woman commented as she picked up her bulging shopping bags so they could sit down.

'It is. It looks as though you've found plenty of things to buy,' Catherine observed lightly.

'Oh, I always do.' The woman laughed as she glanced at Hannah. The child was busily arranging the teddies on one of the chairs so that they could join in the tea party. 'I see your little girl has had a good day, too!'

'Oh, but she isn't…' Catherine didn't get the chance to correct her as the woman moved away. Hannah giggled and she turned to look at her. 'That lady thought you were my mummy, didn't she, Catherine?'

'She did.' Catherine summoned a smile, hoping the comment hadn't upset the little girl. Did Hannah miss not having a mother? she found herself wondering.

'I wish you were my mummy, Catherine. Then you'd be able to come out with us all the time and read me bedtime stories every night.' Hannah smiled trustingly up at her. 'Wouldn't you like to be my mummy? 'Cos if you want to, we can ask Daddy if he'd mind.'

'I…um…' Catherine was at a loss to know what to say. She didn't have enough experience of children to know how to explain that it wasn't quite that simple. She heaved a sigh of relief when she spotted Matt and Becky coming back with their tea. 'Oh, look, here's Becky and your daddy and they've bought some lovely cakes for our tea.'

Hannah was successfully distracted. Catherine helped Matt unload the tray and joined in the conversation as best she could, but the idea kept niggling away at her. Would

Matt have objected if Hannah had put the suggestion to him?

It was the craziest idea in the world but she couldn't get it out of her head. What made it worse was the fact that she was pretty sure that Matt wouldn't have minded one little bit.

They did their shopping after they'd finished their tea. Catherine bought some wrapping paper and Christmas cards from Becky's stall. The cards had been designed by the children in Becky's year and printed on the school's computers. She was impressed by the high standard of the artwork and especially by Becky's contribution.

'It's absolutely lovely,' she said sincerely, studying the beautifully drawn pattern of bells and garlands. Becky had used true Christmas colours and the card was a feast of rich reds and greens. 'You really are clever, Becky. I wish I could draw like that.'

'Becky has always been artistic. She gets it from her mother. Ruth was a commercial artist,' Matt explained, ruffling his daughter's hair in a show of fatherly pride.

'Well, she has real talent. Are you thinking of becoming an artist, Becky?' she began, but before the child could answer there was a sudden commotion by the door. They all turned to watch what was happening and, as the crowd parted, Catherine saw a figure slumped on the floor.

'That doesn't look too good,' Matt said worriedly, turning to her. 'Shall we see if we can help?'

'Yes, of course.'

'You two stay here,' he ordered the children. 'Becky, you're in charge and you're to keep hold of Hannah's hand until we get back.'

He hurried across the room when Becky nodded, and Catherine followed him. The man was slumped against the wall and clutching his chest. He seemed to be having problems breathing so Catherine knelt down and quickly undid his shirt collar.

'Can you hear me?' Matt had knelt beside the man. 'I'm a doctor—can you tell me your name?' He glanced at her when he got no reply. 'See if anyone knows who he is and if he's got a medical history, can you?'

Catherine didn't waste any time as she stood up and turned to address the crowd. 'Does anyone know who this gentleman is?'

'It's Mr Sykes.' One of the teachers who had been supervising the day's proceedings pushed her way to the front of the crowd. 'He's our caretaker.'

'I see. And do you know if he's been ill recently or receiving any medical treatment?' Catherine asked her.

'I've no idea.' The young woman shrugged. 'I only started here this term. Maybe one of the other teachers would know.'

'See if you can find out, will you?' Catherine instructed. 'And will you call an ambulance, please?'

Matt looked round as she knelt beside him. 'Probable heart attack. Classic signs—severe chest pain, cyanosis…'

'And a very rapid and weak pulse,' she added, checking the man's pulse.

'I don't like the look of him at all. His breathing is getting worse.' Matt was oblivious to the crowd that had gathered around them, his whole concentration focused on the patient. There was no doubt that he was a first-rate doctor, Catherine thought admiringly, and suddenly realised that she was glad she'd taken the job at Brookdale Surgery despite her initial reservations.

'He's arrested. Help me lay him down.' There wasn't a trace of panic in Matt's voice as he took charge of the situation. They quickly laid Mr Sykes flat on the floor and Matt checked that the man's heart had stopped beating by placing his fingers against the carotid artery.

He shook his head. 'Nothing. We need to start CPR if he's to have a chance of surviving. You handle the breathing and I'll do the compressions.'

Catherine didn't waste any time. Tipping back the man's

GET FREE BOOKS and a FREE MYSTERY GIFT WHEN YOU PLAY THE...

SLOT MACHINE GAME!

Just scratch off the silver box with a coin. Then check below to see the gifts you get!

YES! I have scratched off the silver box. Please send me the four FREE books and mystery gift for which I qualify. I understand I am under no obligation to purchase any books, as explained on the back of this card. I am over 18 years of age.

M3KI

Mrs/Miss/Ms/Mr _____ Initials _____

BLOCK CAPITALS PLEASE

Surname _____

Address _____

_____

_____ Postcode _____

 Worth FOUR FREE BOOKS plus a BONUS Mystery Gift!

Worth FOUR FREE BOOKS!

Worth ONE FREE BOOK!

TRY AGAIN!

Visit us online at www.millsandboon.co.uk

THE READER SERVICE™
FREE BOOK OFFER
FREEPOST CN81
CROYDON
CR9 3WZ

NO STAMP
NECESSARY
IF POSTED IN
THE U.K. OR N.I.

head, she opened his airway with four sharp inflations then checked to see if his heart had started beating. There was still no sign of a pulse so Matt performed five chest compressions by pressing down on the lower half of the man's breastbone. As soon as he'd finished, Catherine breathed into Mr Sykes's mouth once more, using just a single inflation this time. She and Matt quickly slipped into the familiar rhythm of five compressions followed by one breath. The crowd fell silent as they watched the drama unfolding. Catherine had seen this reaction before and understood. It came as a shock to realise one's own mortality, although hopefully they would be able to keep the caretaker alive long enough for the ambulance to get there.

Fifteen minutes later, they handed over their patient to the paramedics. Catherine sighed as she watched the stretcher being wheeled out of the school hall. It was always a strain having to deal with this type of a situation, but at least the caretaker had a chance of pulling through now that he was on his way to the coronary care centre.

'Fingers crossed he makes it,' Matt said, echoing her thoughts.

The headmaster came over to thank them for their help so it was another few minutes before they could go back to the children. Becky was fine but Hannah seemed to be a bit upset by what had happened.

'Is that man going to go to heaven, Daddy?' she asked, her lower lip wobbling.

Matt swung her up into his arms and hugged her. 'I don't think so, sweetheart. He'll be fine once he gets to the hospital and the doctors and nurses are all there to look after him.'

'My mummy went to hospital, didn't she? And she didn't get better.'

'That's right, but Mummy was very, very sick and the doctors and nurses didn't have any medicine that could make her better.'

Matt's tone was gentle and Catherine felt a lump come

to her throat. She could imagine how hard it must be for him to have to deal with the child's questions. He must have loved his wife an awful lot, she thought, then wondered why it hurt so much to think about him loving another woman.

'I wish she wasn't in heaven 'cos I'd like a mummy.' Hannah suddenly turned and smiled at her. 'You said that you'd be my mummy if Daddy didn't mind. Shall we ask him now, Catherine?'

CHAPTER SEVEN

'MAYBE we should talk about this later, poppet. It's getting late and Granny will be wondering where we've got to.'

It was Matt who smoothly changed the subject. Catherine's cheeks were flaming as she followed him and the girls out of the hall. She had no idea what he was thinking but she knew how she felt. Mortified was the word that best summed it up—completely and utterly mortified!

He ushered the children into the car then opened the passenger door for her but she hung back. The thought of having to sit beside him and make polite conversation on the drive home was more than she could bear. 'I can make my own way home from here. It's not far and there's no point taking you out of your way,' she said stiffly, avoiding his eyes.

'It isn't a problem,' he said smoothly.

Catherine bit her lip. She desperately didn't want him driving her home but she couldn't think of a way to get out of it without causing a scene.

'Look, Catherine, I can see that you're embarrassed about what just happened but there really isn't any need.' Matt smiled when she looked warily at him. 'I know what Hannah is like. Once she gets something into her head then there's no stopping her.'

'I didn't say anything to…well, to make her think that I wanted to…to….' She tailed off, wishing that she hadn't tried to explain because she was only making matters worse.

'I know.' Matt rested his arm on the roof of the car as he regarded her sombrely. 'I couldn't imagine in my wildest dreams that I'd be lucky enough to have you offer to become Hannah and Becky's mother. Let's just put it down to a child's overly fertile imagination and leave it at that, shall we?'

Catherine's heart bounced against her ribs. Had Matt really meant that he would have welcomed her making such an offer, or had it been just a polite way to spare her any further embarrassment?

All of a sudden she couldn't bear to stand there any longer debating the point. Whether or not Matt would consider himself *lucky* to have her as part of his family wasn't the issue. She should be more concerned about sticking to her decision to not get involved.

'That sounds like the best idea.' She summoned a smile, trying to ignore the painful ache that had settled in her heart. She didn't want to be Hannah's or any other child's mother so there was no point suddenly thinking about what she might be missing.

'Anyway, thanks for bringing me here today, Matt. I really enjoyed it but it's time I was off.' She quickly bent and said goodbye to the girls then stepped away from the car. 'I'll see you in work on Monday. Have a nice weekend.'

'You, too. And thanks for coming with us, Catherine. We enjoyed your company.'

Matt didn't press her again to accept a lift. He closed the passenger door and walked around the car to get into the driver's side. Catherine made her way towards the gates, turning to wave when he beeped his horn as he drove past. Tears suddenly pricked her eyes but she blinked them away. There was no point wishing that she'd gone with him, and certainly no point wishing that she didn't have to go home to an empty flat. She'd made her decision and that was the end of the matter. Love, marriage and a family might be what a lot of women dreamed of having but they weren't for her.

*   *   *

The next few weeks flew past in a blur. Sometimes Catherine felt as though she had only to blink and another day had rushed by. The surgery was so busy that she and Matt were hard pressed to keep on top of all the work. An outbreak of flu meant that the number of home visits they were called to doubled almost overnight. Most days they ran over time and finished well after the hour they should have done.

In all honesty Catherine was glad of the increased work-load because it meant they were both too busy to think about anything other than necessities. There certainly wasn't time to talk about personal matters, which was a relief. After their visit to the Christmas fair, she had made up her mind that she would stop letting herself get drawn into Matt's family life, although it had proved harder than she'd expected. Many times she found herself wondering what Hannah and Becky were doing, or she would find herself picturing them and Matt at home together. She wasn't sure why it was happening but it was very frustrating.

December was already into its first week when Catherine arrived at the surgery one Thursday morning to find the place in a state of chaos. The phone was ringing and nobody seemed to be making any attempt to answer it. She went straight into the office and found Sharon there on the verge of tears.

'Are you all right?'

'Yes. No. Oh, I don't know!' Sharon wailed.

'Come along now. It can't be that bad.' Catherine put a comforting hand on the young receptionist's shoulder. 'Tell me what's happened.'

'Margaret's got flu and she won't be coming into work. And Matt has had to go out and I don't know when he'll be back. Then, if that wasn't bad enough, Ann just called in to tell me she's going to be late and now the phone just won't stop ringing!'

'What a mess!' Catherine gave the young woman's

shoulder a squeeze. 'It's no wonder you're upset but we'll sort things out, Sharon. Why don't you make us both a cup of coffee while I answer the phone? We can deal with the rest when you come back.'

By the time Sharon came back with two mugs of instant coffee, Catherine had dealt with half a dozen phone calls. She switched the phone over to the answering-machine and turned off the ringer. 'Right, let's take five, shall we? We can't talk if we keep getting interrupted all the time.'

Sharon looked uncertainly at the phone then shrugged. 'Margaret would have a fit but, seeing as she's not here, I don't suppose it matters.'

'You said she's caught this wretched flu that's been going around, so I assume she must have phoned in sick this morning,' Catherine prompted, pleased to see that the young receptionist had rallied.

'Yes. I'd no sooner got here than her husband rang to say that she wouldn't be in. She must feel really bad because she hates being off work.'

Sharon took a fortifying swallow of coffee before continuing her tale of woe. 'Then, before I'd had a chance to sort myself out, Matt came through from the house to tell me that he'd be late for surgery because he had to take his mother to the airport. Apparently, his sister has gone into labour and her husband is away so she's all by herself. Mrs Lewis managed to get a cancellation and is flying out to Toronto this morning.'

'I see.' Catherine frowned. 'It's going to make things very awkward for Matt, having his mother fly over there earlier than expected.'

'S'pose so.' Sharon shrugged, more concerned about her own problems than anyone else's. 'Anyway the next thing was that Ann arrived all in a panic. David Marshall had phoned her because his carer hadn't turned up. She's gone over there to see if he's all right but it means she's going to be late as well and, as luck would have it, she has an early clinic today. I'm just dreading everyone turning up and having to tell them that they'll have to wait. You know how people complain!'

'Well, they'll just have to complain, I'm afraid. We aren't miracle-workers and there's only so much we can do,' Catherine said firmly. 'I suggest that you try to re-schedule appointments for any of Matt's patients who are willing to come later in the week and I'll just have to fit the rest into my list somehow or other.'

'I'll try. But what about Ann? What am I going to do about her patients?' Sharon asked worriedly. 'A couple of them are down for cholesterol tests, which means they've had to fast overnight.'

'Simple. Cross your fingers and hope she isn't too long!'

Catherine left the office as Sharon laughed. At least the receptionist seemed to have got over her panic. Frankly, there wasn't much they could do except deal with the situation the best way they could. Still, they would manage—one way or another.

She went to her room to get ready for the rush and discovered that Matt had left her a note, briefly explaining what Sharon had already told her. She frowned when she got to the end of the message. He hadn't mentioned anything about the children and she couldn't help worrying about how they were coping. Had Matt had time to make arrangements for them?

She knew that she wouldn't rest until she had found out if they were all right. Sharon was busy with the phone so she didn't disturb her. She hurried through to the house and ran up the stairs. Becky was in the sitting room, gathering together her school books, and she smiled when Catherine appeared.

'Oh, hi, Catherine! Did Dad tell you about Gran having to go and see Auntie Cheryl?'

'He left me a note,' Catherine explained. 'I just wanted to see if you and Hannah were all right.'

'Oh, we're fine. Aunt Bet is here.' Becky grimaced and

lowered her voice. 'She's really nice but she does fuss. She even wanted to walk me to school!'

Catherine hid her smile. 'Well, so long as everything is under control...'

She broke off when Hannah came racing into the room. 'Catherine! Have you come to take me to school? Aunt Bet won't mind.' The little girl turned to the elderly woman who had followed her into the room. 'You don't mind if Catherine takes me to school, do you, Aunt Bet?'

'Well, no, not so long as your daddy wouldn't mind, dear.' The old lady smiled ruefully at Catherine. 'In fact, I'd be grateful not to have to walk all that way with my knee being so bad. Bursitis is so very painful, as I'm sure you know.'

The old lady genteelly raised her skirt a couple of inches. Catherine frowned when she saw how swollen her left knee was. 'You really shouldn't be walking around when it's so swollen. Rest is the only thing that will cure it.'

'I know.' Aunt Bet sighed. She was an older version of Matt's mother, although her hair was more silver than blonde. She had the same wonderful smile as her sister and nephew, although Catherine couldn't help noticing how strained it looked that day.

'Matt told me the last time it flared up that I must stay off my feet until the swelling went down, but I just couldn't leave him to cope on his own when Rosemary phoned to tell me she was having to go to Canada.' Aunt Bet sighed. 'Mind you, I don't know how much help I'm going to be because it's such agony trying to walk.'

Catherine came to a swift decision. 'It would be silly to make your knee any worse than it is. Why don't I take Hannah to school and collect her this afternoon? It's my half-day off so it won't be a problem.'

'Yes! Goody, goody, goody!' Hannah cried in delight. She put her arms round Catherine's waist and hugged her then turned to her aunt. 'And you don't have to worry,

Aunt Bet, 'cos Daddy won't mind a bit. He likes Catherine an awful lot, you see. He told me so.'

Talk about out of the mouths of babes! Catherine thought, feeling her face suffuse with colour.

'In that case, I shall *happily* accept your offer, my dear.' Bet's smile was distinctly coy. 'I feel a lot better knowing that you have Matt's full approval.'

'Er…yes.' Catherine managed to smile back but she couldn't ignore the speculative look the older woman gave her, although it wasn't surprising after what Hannah had said.

All of a sudden her blood started to fizz with excitement. It felt rather good to know that Matt liked her 'a lot'.

It was a busy morning and Catherine was rushed off her feet. Fortunately, most people were sympathetic when they found out that Matt had been called away on a family emergency so there were few complaints about the delay. Catherine dealt with everyone as quickly as she could but there was still a queue in the waiting room when Lauren Hoskins tapped on her door. One look at the troubled expression on Lauren's face was enough to tell her that this was one patient who wouldn't be quickly dealt with.

'Do sit down, Mrs Hoskins.' Catherine waited until the woman had taken a seat. 'So what can I do for you today? Have you had a repeat of your earlier problems and been feeling dizzy again?'

'It's not just dizziness now. I keep getting these pains as well—right here.' Lauren pressed a hand to her chest.

Catherine frowned. The ECG results hadn't shown any problems with Lauren's heart but she couldn't take any chances. 'I think I should examine you again, Mrs Hoskins. Would you pop behind the screen and take off your blouse?'

She gave Lauren a few minutes to get ready then opened the screen and discovered that the woman was perched on the edge of the couch, sobbing her heart out.

'Why don't you tell me what's wrong?' she said quietly, plucking a tissue out of the box on the shelf and handing it to Lauren.

'Everything! It's all gone wrong and I don't know what to do or how we're going to manage!'

Lauren began to sob even harder. Catherine took hold of her hand and held it. 'Problems are rarely as bad as we think they are. Why don't you tell me all about it? I suspect that the real reason why you've been feeling so ill recently is because of what has been happening in your life.'

It all came tumbling out after that. Catherine listened with mounting sympathy as Lauren told her how her husband had lost his job and how they were having difficulty paying their bills without his salary. They had taken out a huge mortgage when they had bought their house and they were behind with the repayments and were being threatened with repossession. It had been a doubly bitter blow because they'd bought the house so they could start a family and now they'd had to give up the idea because they couldn't afford Lauren to leave work.

Lauren took a wobbly breath as she came to the end of her tale. 'I just don't know where to turn. I lie awake at night, worrying about what is going to happen to us.'

'It's no wonder you've been feeling ill,' Catherine observed. 'You're suffering from stress, Lauren, and that's why you had those dizzy spells and now have pains in your chest.'

'But I didn't imagine it! I really did feel dizzy and the pains I had were definitely real, Dr Lewis. I honestly thought I was having a heart attack!' Lauren declared, sounding upset.

'I know they were real. Stress can and does cause very *real* physical symptoms,' Catherine assured her. 'People can suffer horrendously from stress-related symptoms such as palpitations, muscular pains or feelings of anxiety.'

'Oh, I see. I thought you were trying to say that it was all in my mind.'

'Not at all. Stress is one of the scourges of modern life, I'm afraid. Although most people don't realise it, the problems they encounter on a daily basis can have a marked effect on their health,' she explained. 'There is actually a scoring system which allocates points for various stressful events. Things like moving house, getting divorced, changing—or losing—a job are all known to increase stress levels.'

'And you think that's what's been happening to me? That it's worrying what Peter and I are going to do that has caused me to be so ill lately?' Lauren asked, sounding a little calmer.

'I'm ninety-nine per cent certain that is the cause. However, I want to examine you just to make sure that nothing has been overlooked.'

'I doubt it.' Lauren laughed shakily. 'I think I've had every test in the book in the past few months!' She shook her head. 'I never dreamt it could be worry that was making me feel so dreadful.'

Catherine gave her a thorough examination but once again she could find nothing physically wrong with her. She left Lauren to get dressed, wondering what she could suggest to help Lauren through this difficult period. Until the pressures were removed from her life, it was likely that Lauren would continue to feel ill.

'Is there anything you can give me, Dr Lewis, maybe some tablets to help me cope?' Lauren came and sat down again.

'I'll prescribe a mild antidepressant to help you cope with the anxiety but it isn't a cure.' Catherine chose her words with care. 'The root cause of your problems, Mrs Hoskins, is what is happening in your life. You need to address the situation and see if you can work out a solution. Have you talked it over with your husband and told him how worried you are?'

'No. Peter's been very down lately. Losing his job hit him hard and I didn't want to make things worse. I haven't even told him that I've been feeling ill,' Lauren admitted. 'I've just tried to carry on as normal, to be honest. I deal with all the bills so Peter has no idea just how bad the situation really is.'

'Then your first priority must be to tell him,' Catherine said firmly, thinking to herself that Matt had been right in his assessment. Lauren had been keeping up a front and the pressure had made her ill.

It just went to prove once again how very astute he was. It also made her realise that any woman who was married to Matt would never find herself in the same position as Lauren. Matt would always be there to give his support, rock-solid in a time of crisis.

A shiver ran through her. It wasn't the first time she'd thought that but it seemed to have had a bigger impact this time. It wasn't easy to dismiss the thought that *she* could lean on Matt and that he would always be there if she needed him. It was such a reversal of her usual view that it both shocked and scared her. It would be only too easy to accept it as the truth but what if she were wrong, what if Matt wasn't as steadfast as she assumed him to be?

Her head whirled as the question spun round inside it so that it was an effort to focus on Lauren's problems. 'Obviously, I can only suggest that you talk to your husband, Mrs Hoskins. At the end of the day the decision is yours. But at least promise me that you'll think about what I've said.'

'I suppose I'll have to.' Lauren smiled faintly. 'It's fast reaching the point where Peter is going to find out that something is wrong. I suppose it was silly to keep pretending everything was fine but it isn't easy to let your friends and family know that you've made a mess of your life, is it?'

'I'm sure that nobody will think that. Not if they are real friends, anyway,' Catherine assured her, hoping it was true. 'Now, would you like me to write out that prescription for you?'

'No, thank you.' Lauren sounded much more sure of herself. 'Drugs aren't going to solve the problem, are they? It's time Peter and I faced up to what has happened. Burying your head in the sand only works until the tide comes in!'

Catherine laughed. 'That's one way of putting it. But I'm here if you need to talk to anyone, Mrs Hoskins. Do remember that.'

'I shall. Thank you, Dr Lewis.'

It was a far more confident woman who left the surgery. Catherine was still smiling as she went to press the buzzer to summon her next patient. It was good to know that she had helped...

'It takes a lot of stamina to still be smiling after a morning like you've had.'

She felt her heart jolt when she looked up and saw Matt standing in the doorway. 'Have you just got back?'

'Just this minute. Sharon told me that you've been holding the fort.' He studied her for a moment then shook his head. 'I don't know how you do it.'

'Do what?' she said, thinking how handsome he looked with his hair all mussed from the breeze. He was still wearing his coat and she felt a little shiver ripple through her when it struck her that he must have come straight to find her as soon as he'd arrived.

'Manage to look as cool as a cucumber, of course.' He shook his head. 'I expected to find you looking as though you'd been put through the mill after the morning you've had, but not a bit of it. What's your secret?'

'Oh, some people just rise to the occasion,' she declared airily.

He rolled his eyes. 'That puts me firmly in my place, doesn't it?' He sobered suddenly. 'Joking aside, though, I'm really sorry to have dropped you in at the deep end like that. I take it that you read my note?'

'I did. It must have been a rush for your mother, getting ready to fly out to Canada like that at a moment's notice.'

'It was panic stations, I don't mind telling you.' He glanced round when the phone rang, and grimaced. 'Anyway, I'd better get a move on. I'll speak to you later. OK?'

'Fine.'

Catherine pressed the buzzer as soon as he left. It was only when her next patient arrived that she realised she hadn't told Matt that she was collecting Hannah from school that afternoon. She made a note to tell him later then smiled when she recalled what the little girl had said about her daddy liking her a lot. Was it any wonder that she seemed to be coping so well with all the problems after a boost like that?

CHAPTER EIGHT

'SORRY to bother you, Catherine, but I wondered if I could have a word.'

Surgery had just ended and Catherine was clearing up when Ann Talbot knocked on her door. She put down the notes she'd been holding and beckoned the older woman into the room.

'Come in, Ann. Actually, I was hoping I'd get the chance to speak to you. How's David?'

'Not too good, I'm afraid.' Ann sighed as she closed the door. 'That's why I wanted to talk to you. I know it's supposed to be your afternoon off, but Matt's still tied up with a patient, plus he's got a list of calls that need doing later.'

'Don't worry about it,' Catherine quickly assured her. 'Sharon told me that you'd had to go and see David because his carer hadn't turned up.'

'That's right.' Ann sat down by the desk. She was an attractive woman in her late forties with softly waving blonde hair and a quiet manner. Catherine knew how highly she was regarded by the patients at Brookdale Surgery. Ann was a skilled professional who did her job with very little fuss so it was all the more surprising to see her looking so flustered that day.

'David was in a terrible state when I got to his house. He'd tried to get himself to the bathroom and had fallen out of his wheelchair. He had a nasty bump on his head from where he'd managed to hit it on the edge of the washbasin.'

'How awful!' Catherine exclaimed. 'Was he badly hurt?'

'More shaken up than anything else. Plus, of course, his pride was badly dented at having to phone me for help.'

There was a wealth of sadness in Ann's voice. Catherine studied her downcast face. 'You're very fond of David, aren't you?' she said gently.

'He's just a patient,' Ann began, then sighed. 'Is it so obvious? Yes, I'm fond of him. More than just fond if you want the truth. After his wife left him David became very despondent and I got into the habit of calling round to see him each day after work. I was worried that he might... well, do something silly.'

'It must have been terribly difficult for him. Finding out that he had motor neurone disease must have been bad enough, but to then go through the trauma of his wife leaving must have been a horrendous experience for him.'

'It was. However, David is a fighter and he rallied after a while. I kept visiting him, telling myself that it was just to make sure that he didn't slip back into depression.' Ann laughed sadly. 'It was a lie, of course. I'd fallen in love with him and that's why I wanted to see him.'

'And how does David feel?' Catherine asked quietly.

'I think he feels the same way about me.' Ann stared at the ceiling but Catherine could see that there were tears in her eyes. 'The problem is that he absolutely refuses to discuss the possibility of us having a relationship. He says that he's going to die and that there's no point thinking about the future.'

'But there's no knowing how long he has left,' Catherine protested. 'He could have several years.'

'Or he could have just a few months.' Ann took a tissue from her pocket and wiped her eyes. 'Nobody knows for sure, do they? But it doesn't matter to me if it's months or years because I just want the chance to be with him. At least I'll have something to look back on when the inevitable happens.'

'Is there no way that you can make him see how foolish

he's being?' Catherine asked, thinking how brave Ann was.

'I've tried, believe me, but he's so stubborn!' Ann gave her a wobbly smile. 'I'm sorry, Catherine. I didn't mean to offload all that onto you. What I really came to ask was if you would get onto the care agency. Apparently, his usual carer is off sick with this wretched flu and the agency forgot to arrange for a replacement to visit him. I've phoned their office and read them the Riot Act but it would have a lot more clout coming from you. David could have been lying on the bathroom floor all day if he hadn't had his mobile phone with him and my number programmed into it.'

'I'll certainly phone them. It's unforgivable that he was left to fend for himself. I take it there was someone there when you left him?' Catherine asked worriedly.

'Yes. The agency managed to find someone to cover. To be honest, it's reached a point where he needs twenty-four-hour care, but he refuses to have anyone living in the house. He says that he doesn't need a nursemaid!'

'It's understandable,' Catherine pointed out, although she could understand why Ann was so worried. 'It must be hard to accept that you can no longer be totally independent.'

'I suppose you're right. But I just wish he'd see sense!'

Catherine laughed. 'Maybe you'll just have to try harder to convince him that he's making a mistake by pushing you away. You have my full permission to tell him that I think he's an idiot for not realising how lucky he is to have someone you like you to worry about him.'

'I might just do that!' Ann laughed. 'He can only tell me to get lost and that can't make me feel any worse than I've felt these past six months.'

Catherine sighed as Ann left the room. Wouldn't it be wonderful if Ann *did* manage to make David see sense? So maybe there was a chance that Ann might get hurt but surely it was worth taking that risk?

She frowned because it was completely out of character for her to think like that. Normally she would be the last person to advise anyone to take a risk but she really did believe in this instance that it would be worth it if Ann succeeded in winning David over.

It struck her then just how much she had changed in the short time she'd been working at Brookdale Surgery. Ideas which would have been alien to her now felt quite natural. What had brought about such a massive change in her thinking?

Unbidden, the image of Matt's face sprang to mind and she sighed. Matthew Fielding had an awful lot to answer for!

The school playground was crowded with parents when Catherine arrived to collect Hannah that afternoon. She went and stood near the main doors so the child would see her when she came out. Matt had left the surgery by the time she'd finished talking to Ann so she'd not had a chance to tell him about the new arrangements. She'd toyed with the idea of texting a message to his mobile phone but decided not to bother him in the end. She'd seen the list of calls he had to do that afternoon and there was no point worrying him when there was no need. So long as Hannah was safely delivered home then there wouldn't be a problem.

Hannah was delighted to see her. She skipped along beside her, chattering nineteen to the dozen about all the things she'd done at school that day. Apparently, there was a carol concert being held the following week and Hannah's class was singing 'Away In a Manger'. She insisted on practising the words as they headed back to the surgery, bringing an unexpected lump to Catherine's throat as she unselfconsciously sang the the lovely old carol in a piping little voice. There was something very special about the innocent joy the child exuded that touched Catherine's heart in a way she would never have expected, so it was little wonder that she was feeling a little edgy when Matt drew up alongside them in his car.

'This is a surprise!' he declared, grinning at them through the open window. 'I expected to find Aunt Bet doing escort duty, not you, Catherine.'

'I'm sorry, I should have told you about the change of plans,' she apologised. 'Your aunt's knee was playing up so I offered to fetch Hannah from school to save her having to walk all the way here.'

'Catherine took me to school this morning, as well,' Hannah put in. 'I told Aunt Bet you wouldn't mind, Daddy. You don't, do you? You told me how much you like Catherine.'

Catherine tried to hide her smile when she saw a wash of colour run up Matt's face but he must have noticed her amusement because he grimaced. 'I did. And I should have known better, shouldn't I?'

Catherine wasn't sure what he meant by that. However, before she could work it out, he got out of the car. 'Hop in. I'll drive you back to the surgery.'

'I may as well get off now that you're here,' she demurred.

'What about your car? Haven't you left it at the surgery?' he reminded her, and she sighed.

'Yes, of course. How silly of me to forget.'

She quickly got into the car while he helped Hannah into the back seat and fastened her seat belt. Matt pulled away from the kerb, glancing at her once they were safely under way.

'I really do appreciate you helping out like this, Catherine. I hope it didn't cause you any problems.'

'Not at all. I wasn't planning on doing anything this afternoon apart from some Christmas shopping, and I can do that any time.'

'Don't!' He groaned. 'I don't even want to *think* about Christmas. I've no idea how I'm going to get everything done. Mum usually sorts it all out but it's down to me this year.'

'Can't your aunt help?' she suggested.

'Aunt Bet always spends Christmas in Scotland with her son and his family. She's travelling up there by train next week and I certainly don't want her to feel that she should change her plans because of me.'

He drew up in front of the surgery and switched off the engine. Hannah got out of the car and ran inside but he didn't follow her right away.

'I shall just have to muddle through. The food's easy enough because Mum has ordered most of it from the local shops, but it's all the other things, like the presents for the girls, which worry me. Becky's at that age where she no longer wants toys and I'm not sure what to buy her. I mean, how does a mere male know what a thirteen-year-old girl likes?'

'It's a problem,' Catherine agreed. 'I imagine Becky's a bit too old to write a letter to Santa Claus and give you a clue.'

'She is, worse luck.' He sighed. 'Life was so much easier when all she wanted was the latest Barbie doll.'

Catherine chuckled. 'I expect most parents feel that way when their children are growing up.'

'I expect they do.' He grimaced. 'Sorry. I didn't mean to make it sound as though I'm complaining about my lot.'

'You didn't,' she said firmly. 'It's natural that you should want to give the girls a lovely Christmas, and only natural that you should be worried about how you will cope in the circumstances.'

'I suppose so. Still, that's enough about my problems. How about a cup of coffee before you shoot off?'

It was on the tip of her tongue to accept when Catherine realised that she really should call a halt. She'd already become far more involved in Matt's affairs than she should have done. At the end of the day he had his life to lead and she had hers. For some reason the thought was extremely painful.

'I'll give it a miss if you don't mind,' she said lightly, not wanting him to think there was anything wrong. Not that there was a problem, she hastily assured herself. She was simply sticking to the decision she'd made. Although she enjoyed working at Brookdale Surgery it *was* only a temporary arrangement. Her future was all mapped out and there wasn't enough room in it for a widower and his two children, no matter how appealing the three of them were.

'Sure I can't tempt you?'

His tone was light enough as he tried to persuade her yet Catherine felt a prickle of heat run under her skin when she heard the nuance it held. Her eyes rose to his then skittered away when she saw the knowing gleam they held. Did Matt suspect just how very *tempted* she was? she wondered, then cut short that dangerous thought.

'Another time, perhaps,' she replied politely, opening the car door. 'I want to pop round to see how Mrs Grimes is getting on. Her leg is taking a long time to heal and I know it's still very painful.'

'It's often the case with an elderly person. Sadly, the body loses its ability to heal as one gets older. Still, I won't keep you if you want to get off. Thanks again for everything you've done, Cathy.'

Before she guessed his intentions, he leant over and dropped a kiss on her cheek. Catherine felt her breath catch and stared at him in confusion. He smiled at her, an oddly tender light in his eyes as he brushed his knuckles over the place his lips had touched.

'Drive carefully. The traffic is horrendous at this time of the day.'

'I...I will.' She was so choked with emotion that the words seemed to stick in her throat. Matt gave her another gentle smile then got out of the car.

Catherine took a deep breath as she got out but it didn't seem to achieve very much. She barely noticed when Matt locked the car and headed inside. Her hand strayed to her cheek and she felt a frisson run through her when she felt the lingering heat from his lips beneath her fingertips.

A wave of panic suddenly hit her so that her legs were trembling as she went to her own car and got in. Matt's kiss had awoken all sorts of feelings inside her and it scared her to realise just how vulnerable she was around him. It was obvious that he was deeply attracted to her, but she knew in her heart that he would never be content for them just to have an affair. He would want much more than that from her—far more than she was prepared to give.

Tears filled her eyes as she started the engine. What it all came down to was the fact that she just wasn't brave enough to fall in love and give any man that much power over her life.

'Are you sure there isn't anything you need, Mrs Grimes?'

Catherine had done her best to hide her concern since the old lady had let her into the flat. Although it was less than a week since she'd last seen Mrs Grimes, there had been a marked deterioration in her health. She looked alarmingly frail as she sat huddled in the armchair with the cat on her lap.

'I don't need anyone's help,' the old lady stated belligerently. 'I don't need anyone coming in here telling me what I can and can't do!'

'I wouldn't dream of doing that, Mrs Grimes,' Catherine assured her gently, perching on the edge of the lumpy old sofa. 'I know how much you value your independence but we all need a helping hand at times.'

'My Alfred was always helping folk—known for it he was.' The old lady wiped a tear from her eye. 'Had a real soft heart, he had, but he wouldn't let anyone push 'im round. I wish he was here now 'cause he wouldn't 'ave stood for it.'

'Stood for what, Mrs Grimes?' Catherine asked, hating

to see how upset the poor soul was. 'Is it the council again? Are you worried about having to move and part with Timmy?'

Timmy must have recognised his name because he jumped off the old lady's lap and began to twine himself round Catherine's legs. She laughed as she tickled his ears. 'You're an old softie, aren't you?'

'Timmy likes you, Dr Lewis. He don't take kindly to most people but he likes you.'

Whether it was the cat's approval that helped her make up her mind Catherine wasn't sure, but all of a sudden the whole sorry tale came tumbling out. 'It's not the council as such—although it's their fault because they should 'ave found me some place to live before now. No, it's those young 'uns who come here of a night-time. I'm scared to go to sleep because I don't know what they're going to get up to next. They keep breaking into the empty flats and setting them alight, you see, Doctor. I'm terrified that the whole building is going to go up in flames and me and Timmy won't be able to get out.'

'Have you told the police about what's been happening?' Catherine sighed when the old lady shook her head. 'Why ever not? It's dangerous to let this continue and not report it.'

'Because if I tell the police then they'll make me move out and take Timmy off me. I won't let that happen!'

Catherine was at a loss to know what to suggest for the best. 'I'm sure they wouldn't do that,' she said, crossing her fingers. 'Look, will you let me phone them for you and explain what's been going on? You really can't stay here if you're in danger.'

'But where can we go? According to that man from the council they don't 'ave places where you can take a cat.' Mrs Grimes shook her head. 'I ain't going nowhere without my Timmy.'

They hit a complete impasse after that. No matter how hard Catherine tried, she couldn't persuade Mrs Grimes to reconsider. She drove back to the surgery, wondering what she could do to resolve the situation. She hated to think about the old lady being stuck in that flat, scared out of her wits night after night.

Evening surgery was every bit as busy as the morning one had been. Catherine was worn out by the time she took her notes through to the office. It was gone seven, way past the time she should have finished.

'I don't know where they're all coming from,' Matt declared, following her into the room. He tossed a stack of manila folders into the tray. 'I told Sharon to leave the filing until the morning and go home. The poor kid has been run off her feet with Margaret being off sick. I might have to bring in a temporary receptionist if she's off for very long.'

'It might be a good idea.'

'Think so? Then I'll get onto the employment agency in the morning and see if they have anyone available.'

He stood up straight and stretched. Catherine turned away when she saw the muscles in his shoulders ripple. Given her earlier heart-searching, it seemed unwise to let herself enjoy the sight of his muscular body. He gave his shoulders a final roll and groaned.

'I don't know about you but I'm worn out. It's been a hectic day from start to finish.'

'It has.' Catherine stacked her files in the tray. 'How is your sister, by the way? Have you had any news yet?'

'Would you believe it was a false alarm?'

'Really?' She couldn't hide her astonishment and Matt laughed.

'Really! The consultant reckons it was Braxton-Hicks' contractions. Cheryl is mortified although it's not really her fault. She and Mike live some way out of the city,' he explained, 'so when she started having pains I expect she panicked because she was on her own. She phoned the hospital and they advised her to go straight in, which is why she phoned Mum.'

'So your mother went out there early for nothing?'

'Yes and no. Cheryl must feel a lot better knowing that Mum's there. Mike's job takes him away from home a lot of the time and it can't have been easy for her, being on her own.'

'Well, your mother was planning on being there over Christmas anyway.'

'Yes. To be honest, I'm pleased that she and Cheryl are going to have some time together before the baby arrives. They see way too little of one another as it is.'

'Meanwhile, you're going to have to manage as best you can,' Catherine pointed out.

'Yep. I just hope I don't make a complete mess of things.'

'What do you mean?' she asked when she heard the sadness in his voice.

'Oh, nothing. Take no notice. I'm rambling because I'm tired and hungry and want nothing more than to veg out in front of the telly.'

'Sounds as though your evening is going to be as exciting as mine,' she remarked with a chuckle.

'You're more than welcome to keep me company.'

'Oh, I wouldn't dream of spoiling your plans for a quiet night in,' she replied hastily.

'You wouldn't be spoiling them, Catherine. Far from it.'

There was a throbbing note in his voice that made her heart kick in an extra beat. Catherine summoned a smile but it wasn't easy to ignore the way he was looking at her.

'Thanks, but I'd better get myself off home.'

'I'll walk you out, then. I may as well lock up and set the alarms now to save me having to do it later.'

He followed her from the office, waiting while she fetched her coat. Catherine quickly slipped it on, making sure that he didn't get the chance to help her. The memory of what had happened the last time he'd helped her on with her coat was too vivid to take any chances in her present state of mind. She didn't need to feel his fingers brushing her neck while she was so on edge.

'So what's on the agenda when you get home?' he asked, leaning against the wall as he watched her fastening the belt around her waist.

'Nothing much,' she replied, checking that she had her car keys in her pocket. 'I'll probably make myself something to eat and then watch television for a while—if I can stay awake.'

'It's amazing, isn't it?'

'What is?'

'That most people seem to believe a doctor's life is packed full of excitement and glamour when the truth is that it's mainly hard work.' He shook his head, his blue eyes sparkling with laughter, and once again Catherine felt her heart fit in two beats where one would have sufficed. It was difficult to respond when he continued because she couldn't understand why he seemed to have this effect on her.

'Did you ever wonder if you'd chosen the right profession?'

'Not really. How about you?' she asked shortly. It wasn't easy to explain Matt's attraction. Oh, he was good-looking in a craggy kind of a way but he wasn't the most handsome man she'd ever met by a long chalk. And yet there was something about the combination of his rugged looks and his personality that appealed to her on so many different levels.

'No. Do you think we must both be gluttons for punishment?'

Catherine summoned a smile. 'Probably.'

'So that's another thing we have in common, then.'

Matt's tone was husky all of a sudden and she felt her pulse start to race. It felt as though the air was charged with emotion so that the skin on the back of her neck began to prickle. She had no idea what was happening but it scared her. She didn't want to be drawn in like this, couldn't afford to get involved. She had to make it clear that she wasn't interested in anything more than a working relationship.

'Us and ten million other medics, you mean. Right, it's time I was off home and let you enjoy the delights of television.'

She headed for the door, her footsteps slowing when he made no attempt to move out of her way. There was a solemnity about the look he gave her that made her stomach muscles tighten in sudden alarm.

'Why do you do that, Catherine? What are you afraid of?'

'I've no idea what you mean.' She took another step but he still didn't move aside.

'So it isn't a conscious reaction, then? You don't deliberately pull up the drawbridge every time you feel that someone is getting a bit too close for comfort?'

'I don't know what you're talking about, Matt. I was never any good at solving riddles.' She brushed past him and opened the front door. 'I'll see you in the morning. Goodnight.'

'Goodnight, Catherine.'

He didn't try to detain her any longer. Catherine heard the sound of the bolts being drawn as she ran down the steps to her car. She opened the door then glanced back and realised that Matt had already switched off the surgery lights so that the place was in darkness.

She got into the car, trying to ignore the empty ache inside her, the feeling that she had just turned her back on something very special. Matt had nothing to offer her apart from the experience she would gain through working with him. He was just a colleague and he would never be any more than that.

She knew it was true yet, no matter how hard she tried, she couldn't convince herself that she'd done the right thing by walking away from him. Part of her wished that she'd stayed.

CHAPTER NINE

'THIS should clear up the problem. Just make sure that Alison completes the full course of antibiotics, Mrs King. That's most important.'

Catherine handed over the prescription. It was Friday morning and Sandra King had brought in her two-year-old daughter, Alison, to see her. The toddler had been crying all night and it turned out that she had a rather nasty ear infection.

'Thank you, Doctor.' Sandra hefted the little girl into her arms and sighed. 'None of us got a wink of sleep last night. I feel as though I'm walking round in a fog this morning.'

Catherine smiled sympathetically because she understood exactly how the woman felt. She, too, had spent a sleepless night, going over and over everything that had happened before she'd left the surgery. She knew she'd been right to leave when she had. Getting involved with Matt wasn't an option, yet she still couldn't shake off the feeling that she'd made a mistake.

'Then let's hope the antibiotics do the trick,' she said, determinedly returning her thoughts to work. 'How's Benjamin, by the way? His asthma isn't playing him up at the moment, I hope.'

'Oh, he's fine, apart from having a fit of the sulks.' Sandra grimaced. 'We're moving to Hastings on Monday and Benjie is none too thrilled about it. He's upset about having to leave his friends even though I've told him they're welcome to come and stay with us any time they like. Still, I'm sure he'll cheer up once we get there. And it will be a lot better for him living by the sea than in the city.'

'It will,' Catherine agreed. She saw Sandra out then went to the office to check if there was anyone waiting. Although they operated an appointment system, anyone needing to be seen urgently was always fitted in. Surprisingly, there was nobody waiting that day which meant she could finish on time for once. She might even get time for a bit of lunch as well before she did the house calls. Amazingly, there were only two down for that afternoon, which should mean another early finish.

She went back to her room and tidied up. There was an antenatal clinic that afternoon and she knew that Matt would be kept busy seeing to all the expectant mothers. She'd seen the list of patients who were booked in that day and found herself wondering how he would go about collecting Hannah from school. Even though she had promised herself that she wouldn't get involved, she couldn't help worrying how he would manage. Maybe she should offer to cover the clinic while he popped out.

Catherine left her room and walked the short distance along the corridor to tap on his door. She ran a smoothing hand over her hair while she waited for him to answer and was shocked when she realised that she was trembling. All she was doing was offering a colleague helping hand, she told herself sternly. It was what she would do for anyone in the circumstances. However, it was hard to accept that was all it entailed when her heart was beating up a storm. She was on the point of leaving when Matt opened the door.

'Sorry. I was on the phone. Did you want me, Catherine?'

'I...um...I was just wondering if you'd managed to find someone to fetch Hannah from school. You've an antenatal clinic this afternoon and I just thought...'

'Yes! Thank you so much! I've been tearing my hair

out, wondering how I was going to get away from here.'
He grinned at her. 'You're a real star for offering to collect
Hannah. She'll be thrilled.'

'Oh, um, don't mention it.' She took a quick breath but
there was no way she could admit that she hadn't come to
offer her services when she saw the relief on his face. It
struck her all of a sudden just how much pressure he must
be under as he tried to balance the demands of his job
against the needs of his children.

It was that very thought which had convinced her years
ago that having a family was out of the question. Now
Catherine felt a wave of sickness rise inside her when it
hit her afresh how impossible it would be to fulfil her
dream of opening her own practice if she had a family to
care for. It was odd how upsetting she suddenly found it
when the thought of not having children had never bothered her before.

'Damn!'

She looked up when Matt cursed, hoping he couldn't
tell how shocked she felt. To suddenly realise that she was
having doubts about the life she had chosen was unsettling
enough, but to face the fact that the reason for her change
of heart was because of Matt was so much worse. Falling
in love went against everything she had ever believed in,
and falling in love with a man with a ready-made family
would be a complete disaster. It would be so easy to end
up in the same position her mother had been in...

Except that Matt would never let *her* down as her father
had let her mother down, a small voice whispered. He
wasn't that type of a man.

Her head spun as the thoughts whirled inside it but she'd
had years to perfect the art of hiding her feelings and it
stood her in good stead now. 'Is something wrong?'

'I've just remembered that Becky has choir practice after school tonight so she's going to be late getting home.
I was counting on her to look after Hannah, but she won't

be back till five o'clock. There is no way that I can leave Hannah on her own for all that time.'

'What about your aunt? Can she look after Hannah for you?'

'No. I was just speaking to her on the phone when you knocked, in fact. I was hoping that Aunt Bet might be able to fetch Hannah from school if I sent a taxi for her, but it turns out that her knee is worse than ever. I've given her strict instructions that she's got to stay off her feet until the swelling subsides.' He shook his head. 'The only thing I can do is to tell Sharon to cancel some of the antenatal appointments.'

Catherine frowned. She could tell how much he disliked the idea and understood why. It was essential that every expectant mother received regular antenatal care throughout her pregnancy to avoid any possible complications.

'Would it help if I stayed with Hannah until Becky gets home?' she suggested slowly, unable to think of a better solution.

'Oh, no. I can't expect you to do that,' he began, but she didn't let him finish. Maybe she did have doubts about the wisdom of her offer but in her *professional* opinion it was the only solution. There was no way that she could allow her personal feelings to interfere with the welfare of their patients.

'It really isn't a problem, Matt,' she said coolly. 'It would be highly unprofessional to cancel any appointments.'

'In that case, I'll accept your offer. Thank you.'

His tone matched hers and she frowned because she wasn't sure why she had the feeling that he was upset. She shot him a careful look from under her lashes but his expression gave away little about his true feelings. He dug in his pocket and came up with a bunch of keys which he handed to her.

'Here's the keys to the house. I try to keep the children

out of the surgery so let yourself in through the front door. Hannah usually has her tea as soon as she gets home so I'll leave something ready for her.'

'Don't worry. I'll sort it all out.'

She turned away because she didn't want him to see how much it hurt to hear him talk to her in that distant tone. Maybe Matt was only following her lead but she missed hearing the usual warmth in his voice, that special note that he reserved for her alone.

Her heart bumped painfully because up till then she hadn't been conscious of the fact that he spoke to her any differently, but it was true. Maybe that was part of his appeal, the fact that he made her feel so special?

Tears burned her eyes as she slipped the keys into her pocket. In the whole of her life nobody had ever made feel really special before. Oh, she'd always striven to be the best at everything she did: top of her class at school; the student with the highest marks in college; the most promising trainee during her postgraduate studies. However, nobody had ever made her feel as though she was number one just because she was herself. Matt did, though. She didn't need to be anyone in his eyes other than Catherine.

'Thanks again, Catherine. I really appreciate this. If you have any problems, just come and get me.'

'We'll be fine, Matt.' She looked up and there was no way that she could pretend at that moment because she didn't have the strength to lie to herself. If she was special to Matt then he was just as special to her. 'You don't need to worry about Hannah because I'll look after her.'

'I know you will.'

His tone was suddenly filled with all the warmth and tenderness that had been missing before. Catherine felt her heart swell with sudden happiness. She had the craziest urge to tell him how good it felt to have him talk to her that way again but she couldn't do that. It went way beyond the boundaries she had lived within for all these years and she was too scared to go that far. Even though she knew in her heart that Matt was very different from her father, the fear of being let down was still too strong.

'Oh, by the way, I had a phone call from the housing officer first thing this morning about Mrs Grimes. Apparently, they've found a flat for her in a sheltered housing complex on the outskirts of the city.'

'What about her cat? Can she take it with her?' she put in quickly, not wanting to dwell on such unsettling thoughts because it didn't seem to help.

'Yes. That's the really good news. Mrs Grimes has already looked at the flat and it meets with her approval. With a bit of luck she should be rehoused before Christmas.'

'That's great. It's such a relief to know that she's got somewhere safe to live at last.'

'It is.' His tone softened. 'I know how worried you were about her, Catherine.'

Catherine didn't say anything although it was disconcerting to admit that Matt was right. She *had* been worried about the old lady and it just seemed to highlight once again how much her attitude had changed since she'd started working at the surgery.

She left his office and went back to her room to finish tidying up then went for lunch. There was a bistro further along the road so she decided to go there for a treat. The food was good and the atmosphere was convivial yet she derived very little enjoyment from her solitary meal. Sitting there on her own just made her feel lonely.

She tried to shed her sombre mood by reminding herself of all the good things about her life. She was a successful doctor on her way to achieving her dream of opening her own practice. She had a beautiful flat, a nice car and plenty of lovely clothes. A lot of women would be thrilled to trade places with her.

Nevertheless, as she sat there, listing all the things she

had to be grateful for, she couldn't ignore the negative aspects of her life. She did have a beautiful flat but she lived there *on her own*. When she drove her car, there was *nobody* sitting in the seat beside her. And as for all the beautiful clothes hanging in her wardrobe, when was the last time *anyone* had paid her compliment about how she looked?

What it all came down to was that she was a woman on her own, and it scared her to think of all the lonely years ahead. Did she want to end up like poor Mrs Grimes with just a cat for company? Yet what was the alternative? Was she really prepared to give up everything she'd worked so hard to achieve for the sake of love?

She paid her bill and left the restaurant. Her car was still parked at the surgery so she went back to fetch it so she could do the house calls. It wasn't far to the first address and within a few minutes she was drawing up outside. Switching off the engine, she reached for her case and suddenly caught sight of herself in the rear-view mirror.

A shiver ran through her when she saw the uncertainty in her brown eyes. She hadn't answered the question about whether or not she would give up everything for love because she was no longer sure what the answer should be. A few weeks ago she wouldn't have had to think about it, but that had been before she'd met Matt. Now she couldn't put her hand on her heart and swear that she would never fall in love, and the thought of what it could mean scared her. Would Matt really be enough to compensate for having to forfeit her dreams?

Catherine had ample time to get her calls done before she needed to collect Hannah from school. The little girl was delighted when she saw her standing in the playground, and came running straight over to her.

'My teacher said you were coming, Catherine! Daddy phoned and told her that you'd be here to meet me.'

'Did he indeed?' Catherine chuckled. It was hard to remain aloof in the face of the child's enthusiasm. 'And there I was hoping I'd be able to surprise you.'

'Oh, it was still a surprise!' Hannah assured her, slipping her hand into Catherine's as they left the playground. 'I really like it when you come to fetch me. I love Granny, but I can pretend that I have a real mummy like all the other boys and girls when you come for me.'

Catherine wasn't sure what to say to that. The admission had touched her deeply but she didn't want Hannah getting the wrong idea. She sighed because there wasn't an easy way to explain to the child the true nature of the situation when she had such difficulty understanding it herself.

The *old* Catherine would never have dreamt of collecting Hannah from school. It wouldn't have crossed her mind to worry about the problems Matt might be experiencing, juggling his work and his family. She would have done her job and that would have been the sum total of her input. It just went to prove the effect he had on her and that, of course, opened the floodgates to some more in-depth soul-searching. It was a good job that Hannah didn't seem to need her input and chattered away as they made their way back to the house.

'Take off your coat and put it away then we can see what Daddy has left for your tea,' Catherine instructed after she had let them in.

'OK!'

Hannah went shooting off up the hall and bundled her coat into the cupboard under the stairs. Catherine shook her head as she went after her and hung it on a peg.

'It will be creased to rags if you don't hang it up, madam.'

'That's what Daddy calls me—a little madam.' Hannah

laughed as she followed Catherine to the kitchen. 'He also calls me his little monkey.'

'Very apt,' she replied dryly, looking round. There was no sign of a note so she went to the fridge, hoping that Matt might have left Hannah's tea in there, but once again drew a blank. She closed the fridge, wondering if she should go through to the surgery and ask him what she should give Hannah, but it didn't seem worth making a fuss.

'I don't think your daddy has had time to make your tea so what would you like to eat?'

'Fish fingers and chips,' Hannah replied promptly. She ran to the freezer and took out a packet of fish fingers and a bag of oven chips.

'Right, fish fingers and chips it is.' Catherine agreed, then cast an uncertain look at the solid-fuel range. 'That's if I can work out how to use this monstrosity.'

'Daddy puts the chips and fish fingers in the oven,' Hannah explained helpfully.

'Well, that sounds simple enough.' Catherine opened the oven door and peered inside, drawing back when a blast of heat hit her.

'Can I watch television, please?' Hannah asked.

'Yes, of course,' she replied distractedly, wondering if the oven was too hot. There didn't seem to be any way to adjust the temperature, however, so she found a tray and put the fish and chips on it while Hannah went upstairs. She checked her watch after she closed the oven door. It would take at least twenty minutes before the food was ready so she may as well go upstairs and watch television as well.

Hannah had found a cartoon on the children's channel so they sat on the sofa and watched it together. It had been years since Catherine had seen any children's programmes and she soon found herself laughing at the cartoon characters' antics. They were both engrossed when she suddenly heard a shrieking noise coming from downstairs.

'What on earth is that?' she began, then gasped in dismay. 'It's the smoke alarm! Come along, Hannah. Be quick now.'

She bustled the child out of the sitting room and down the stairs. Clouds of black smoke were billowing out of the kitchen so she hurried the little girl along the hall, wanting to be sure she was safe before she went to investigate. Matt met them at the front door. She could see Sharon and a couple of patients standing in the drive and realised that he must have evacuated the surgery when he'd heard the alarm ringing.

'What's happened?'

'I don't know but there's smoke coming out of the kitchen.'

'Stay there and I'll take a look,' he instructed, hurrying into the house.

Catherine waited outside, her heart racing as she wondered if she should have stopped him going back inside. One read such terrible stories about people being trapped in blazing houses. What if he was overcome by smoke? she thought sickly. He might not be able to get out of the house in time.

'Looks like I've found the culprit.'

Matt came back, carrying a blackened tray. Catherine stared incredulously at the charred remains of Hannah's tea. 'You mean all that smoke came from a couple of fish fingers and a few chips?'

'Yep, looks like it.'

She heard the amusement in his voice and a wave of embarrassed heat rushed up her face. 'I'm really sorry, Matt! I just don't know what to say. I've never used an oven like that before and had no idea the food would cook so quickly.'

'It's not your fault, Catherine. That stove is difficult to

use if you're not used to it.' He touched her lightly on the arm and she saw the tenderness in his gaze. 'So long as nobody was hurt, it really doesn't matter, does it?'

'No,' she agreed, although her heart was hammering so fast that it was difficult to form even that single word. She took a quick breath when Sharon came over to ask if it was safe to go back into the surgery. Matt asked her to take the patients back inside then told Hannah she could go back into the house.

'Catherine will be along very shortly,' he assured the child when she hung back. 'I just want to have a word with her first.'

'You won't tell her off, will you, Daddy?' Hannah said anxiously.

'Of course not! Although Catherine might tell me off for not leaving your tea ready as I promised to do.'

Hannah giggled as she ran back inside. Matt sighed as he turned to Catherine. 'Joking aside, I really wouldn't blame you if you did tell me off. I am truly sorry that you had such a fright when you were trying to do me a favour.'

'Some favour! I almost burnt down your house.'

'Stop exaggerating. There was never any danger of the house burning down. And, as I said, it was my fault for not leaving everything ready for you. I had a problem with one of my expectant mums,' he explained. 'Her blood pressure was sky high and I decided that she needed to see her consultant a.s.a.p. By the time I'd phoned the hospital and sorted everything out, it had gone right out of my head.'

'It's understandable. You can't remember everything, Matt. You aren't Superman.'

'Oh, I'm well aware of that!' He grimaced. 'I thought it would be easier to manage as the girls got older but I still find myself having to juggle work and home, I'm afraid.'

'It's usually the case. That's why I decided a long time

ago that I would never have a family.' The admission slid
out before she could stop it, and she saw him frown.

'That sounds a very drastic decision to have made,
Catherine. Are you sure you won't come to regret it?'

'No. I know what I want from life and children simply
don't feature on my list of priorities.'

She swiftly changed the subject because she really
didn't want to discuss her decision when she was feeling
so ambivalent. Something warned her that Matt could be
extremely persuasive if he set his mind to it and she knew
it would be a mistake to let him talk her round and maybe
come to regret it. 'I'd better go and see what Hannah is
up to. Do you want me to find something else for her tea
or would you rather not to risk letting me loose in your
kitchen again?'

'Oh, I think I can trust you, Catherine. I doubt if you
will cause too much damage—to my house at least.'

She wasn't sure what he had meant by that rather cryptic
remark and before she could ask him to explain, Sharon
poked her head round the door.

'Mrs Tate wants to know if she should wait, Dr Fielding.
She needs to collect her little boy from the child-minder's
house in half an hour.'

'Tell her I'll be straight there, will you, Sharon?' He
turned to Catherine as the receptionist hurried away. 'I'd
better get back. Becky should be home soon so she can
look after Hannah then.'

'I'll hang on until she gets here,' she assured him.

'Thanks. Oh, you'd better have this.' He grinned as he
handed her the burnt tray. 'I think the bin is the best place
for it, don't you?'

Catherine went inside as he hurried back to his patients.
The smoke had cleared now and she was relieved to see
that there had been no real damage caused to the kitchen.
She deposited the ruined tray in the waste bin then set
about making something for Hannah to eat, opting for

sandwiches rather than chancing her luck with the stove a second time. Becky arrived just as she had finished buttering the bread and looked surprised to see her.

Catherine explained why she was there, wryly confessing about her mishap with the oven to the girl's amusement. She finished making the sandwiches then left Becky in charge and went through to the surgery and discovered that her first patient had already arrived. She told Sharon to give her a couple of minutes and went to get ready.

It had been a busy afternoon, she thought, taking a prescription pad from the drawer. First the house calls then the trip to school to collect Hannah. The least said about her disaster in the kitchen the better but it had given her an insight into what Matt had to contend with each day. His life must be a constant battle to balance home and work. Still, she'd really rather enjoyed it. It had felt good to be useful. In fact, she wouldn't mind helping him again if he was ever stuck.

A frown pleated her brow because the last thing she should be doing was planning on getting more deeply involved with Matt's family.

Evening surgery was extremely busy and Catherine was glad that she'd managed to get an early start. She worked her way through her list then added on another couple of patients who had turned up without an appointment. One was a young woman who was threatening to miscarry. Sadly there was very little she could to for her patient so she phoned for an ambulance to take the woman to hospital. It was six-thirty by the time the ambulance left and Matt had just finished. He joined Catherine at the front door as she watched the paramedics driving away.

'Problems?'

'A young woman threatening to miscarry,' she explained, turning to go back inside.

'Oh? What's her name?'

'Deborah Hale.'

'What rotten luck!' he exclaimed as she closed the door. 'Debbie was over the moon when I confirmed that she was pregnant. She must be—what—nine or ten weeks by now?'

'Nine,' she confirmed, heading back to her room. 'She said she'd been feeling fine until about an hour ago when she suddenly started having stomach cramps and realised she was bleeding. She got her husband to bring her straight here but there wasn't a lot I could do.'

'There's not much anyone can do in that situation. It's a case of letting nature take its course, although it's hard for any woman to accept that. Ruth had a miscarriage and she was dreadfully upset. I think that's why she was so determined to go through with her pregnancy when she found out she was expecting Hannah.'

He paused when the phone rang. Catherine was glad of the interruption because she had no idea what to say. How different Matt's life might have been if his wife hadn't been taken from him, she thought.

It was a sobering thought and she was happy not to dwell on it when Sharon popped her head round the door. 'It's Ann Talbot, Dr Fielding. She says that she needs to speak to you urgently. It sounds as though she's in a real panic, too.'

'I wonder what's happened,' Matt exclaimed as he hurried to the office.

Catherine quickly followed. It was obvious that it was something serious because she could tell how concerned he was when he came off the phone.

'David Marshall's having trouble breathing. Ann thinks he needs to go to hospital but he won't let her phone for an ambulance. She wants me to go round there and try to persuade him to see sense.'

He hurried to his room to fetch his bag and Catherine went after him. 'Is there anything I can do to help?'

'I can't think of anything... Oh, I know. Will you go through to the house and tell Becky and Hannah to put their coats on?'

'Of course.' She turned to leave then paused. 'Surely you aren't going to take the girls with you?'

'I don't have a choice. I can't leave them here on their own. They'll be perfectly all right in the car. There's no need to worry, Catherine.'

Maybe there wasn't but she couldn't help it. It seemed wrong to take the children out at that time of the night and wrong to expect Matt to do his job and look after them as well. She came to a swift decision.

'I'll stay here with the girls while you go to see David. If you do manage to talk him into going to hospital, Ann will probably need your support.'

'I really don't expect you to keep covering for me, Catherine.'

'I know you don't.' She smiled when she saw the doubt on his face. 'I wouldn't offer if I didn't want to do this, Matt. That's the truth!'

'Then thank you very much because I accept.' He picked up his bag and hurried to the door then paused when he drew level with her. 'Tell the kids I'll be as quick as I can, will you?'

'I will. Don't worry. We'll be fine.' She made a cross over her heart and grinned up at him. 'I promise on my honour that I shall stay out of your kitchen, too, so you don't need to worry about that!'

'That's the very least of my worries,' he growled, bending to drop a kiss on her lips before he left.

Catherine's head was reeling as she watched him striding along the hall. He opened the front door then glanced back. 'I'll see you later, Catherine.'

'I...I'll be here.'

She heard the husky note in her voice and knew that he'd heard it, too. She took a small breath as the front door closed then another just to prove to herself that she could still do something as simple as breathing. Sharon wished her goodnight as she left, and Catherine answered, or she assumed she did. It was as though all her sensory perceptions had switched themselves off—all except one.

Heat raced through her veins when she recalled the fleeting pressure of Matt's mouth on hers. The kiss had been all too brief but she'd felt the passion it had held. She had promised him that she would stay and there was no way that she could go back on her word. When he got home she would be there in his house, with his children, waiting for him.

She had no idea what would happen then but she wasn't going to pretend that the kiss wouldn't have repercussions. No man could have kissed a woman like Matt had kissed her if he didn't *feel* something for her.

CHAPTER TEN

IT WAS after nine by the time Matt got back. Catherine switched off the television as soon as she heard the front door opening. She had tried her best to stay calm while she'd been waiting for him to return but it wasn't easy to ignore the way her heart was thudding all of a sudden.

'Sorry I was so long.' He dropped his case by the door and came into the room. Catherine frowned when she saw the weariness on his face. He looked worn out although it was hardly surprising after the day he'd had.

'How was David? Did you manage to persuade him to go to hospital in the end?'

'No. He refused point-blank to let us phone for an ambulance or take him there by car.'

He sank down on the sofa and closed his eyes. 'We couldn't force him to go but I'd feel a lot happier if he was safely tucked up in a hospital bed at this precise moment.'

'I'm sure you did everything you could, Matt. What exactly was wrong with him?'

'Pneumonia. It turns out that he hadn't been wholly truthful when he'd told Ann that he'd fallen out of his wheelchair yesterday morning. Apparently, he'd fallen during the previous night while he'd been getting himself a drink of water. He must have knocked himself out because when he came to it was morning. There was no sign of his carer so that's when he phoned Ann.'

'Oh, no! I wonder if he maybe inhaled some of the water when he fell. That could be what has caused his pneumonia.'

'Precisely what I thought, although it doesn't make

much difference now how he got it.' Matt sighed as he opened his eyes. 'Anyway, after a lot of arguing I told him point-blank that I wasn't prepared to leave him in the house on his own so he agreed that Ann could spend the night there. I've dosed him up with some heavy-duty antibiotics and promised Ann that I'll go back with some oxygen in case he needs it. I'm just trying to summon up enough energy to set off again.'

'Do you want me to take it on my way home?' she offered immediately. 'It would save you having to go out again.'

'Would you mind?'

'Of course I don't mind! Anyway, don't forget the girls. You can't go out and leave them here on their own, can you?'

'No, of course not. And I can't expect you to stay here any longer either. I don't know what I'm thinking about.' He grimaced. 'Anyway, I hope they weren't too much trouble.'

'They were as good as gold,' she assured him. 'They're both in bed now so you can put your feet up and have a well-earned rest after I've left.'

She stood up, hoping he couldn't tell how disappointed she was at having the evening cut short. However, there was no way she wanted Matt to go out again that night when he looked so exhausted. 'I'll take the portable oxygen tank out of the treatment room, shall I?'

'You may as well. There's a spare one in the supplies cupboard but I don't feel like digging around in there at this precise moment to find it.' He shook his head. 'I must be getting old. I never used to feel *this* tired at the end of the day!'

'Rubbish! You're not old, just worn out from trying to fit too many things into too few hours.'

'More, more!' he encouraged, grinning at her. 'I don't care if you're only saying that to cheer me up—but I much prefer your diagnosis to my own!'

'It's always best to get a second opinion if you're unsure, Dr Fielding.' She returned his smile, feeling her heart skip a beat when he stood up. There was something about the expression on his face that told he wasn't just going to escort her out of the house. 'Th-they drummed that into us at med school, didn't they?'

'They did, although I've always believed that it depends on who's giving the opinion.' He framed her face between his hands and looked into her eyes. 'It means a lot more coming from you than it would if it came from anyone else.'

'Oh? And why is that?' she whispered, her heart almost leaping out of her chest in its excitement.

'Because your opinion matters, Catherine. Especially when it's about me.'

She knew he was going to kiss her then and just for a moment she was overwhelmed by fear at the thought of what she was getting into. But then his lips found hers and nothing seemed to matter any more.

She wrapped her arms around his neck and pulled his head down so he could deepen the kiss, sighing when she felt his tongue slip inside her mouth. She had been kissed before by other men but she had never experienced a fraction of the feelings that filled her now. Matt's lips were so warm and tender, so hungry and yet so satisfying that both her head and her heart reeled. She was trembling when he drew back and rested his forehead against hers but, then, so was he.

'Wow! As kisses go, that has to be a real mind-blower.' His lips brushed her forehead and she shivered when she felt the feather-light touch on her hot skin.

'It wasn't bad,' she said shakily, not really aware of what she was saying at that moment.

'Not bad?' He drew back and stared at her. 'Not bad! It was a genuine, mind-blowing experience, and you have the cheek to say it was "not bad".'

Catherine giggled when she heard the disgust in his voice. 'All right, then, it was very good. Happy now?'

'I suppose I shall have to be,' he grumbled. 'At least you didn't say it was *nice*. Now that would have been a real passion-killer!'

'Bearing in mind that I'm about to leave, maybe "nice" would have been a better description,' she pointed out with a logic that was dredged from somewhere deep inside her. She needed to bear that thought in mind every bit as much as Matt did, she warned herself.

'You could always come back.'

'Pardon?' It was her turn to stare at him and she felt her breath catch when she saw the expression in his eyes. There was so much hunger there that it felt as though she had never seen such longing on anyone's face before. Matt wanted her as only a man could want a woman he cared very deeply for, and the thought almost blew her away.

'You could come back here after you've taken the oxygen to David.' His voice was as soft and as deep as velvet and she shivered when she felt it caressing her nerves. 'It won't take you very long to deliver it and while you're away I can make us a meal. I don't suppose you've had anything to eat yet, have you?'

'No.' She wet her lips because all of a sudden they felt so dry that it was difficult to speak. Her heart jerked when she saw the hungry way his eyes followed the movement of her tongue.

'Good. I'll open a bottle of wine and after we've eaten we can finish it off while we listen to some music. I find it helps me unwind after a busy day to sit here by the fire with the stereo playing in the background.'

His voice had deepened as he set the scene for her. Catherine closed her eyes so she could picture it in her mind—the meal, the wine, the two of them sitting together in front of the fire...

'And after we've finished the wine, we can decide what we want to do next.'

'Next?'

Her breath caught as the next scene began to unwind inside her head. A shudder ran through her as she imagined him bending over her, kissing her and stroking her skin before he picked her up in his arms and carried her up the stairs to his bed. The pictures were so vivid, so real that it was hard to believe that it was happening only in her imagination.

'Mmm. I know what *I* want to happen, Catherine, but I won't press you into doing something you might regret.' He took a deep breath but his voice was hoarse when he continued, filled with a passion and need that made her whole body tingle.

'I want you to stay the night here with me, but if it's not what you want then I'll understand. Don't let me talk you into doing something that you feel in your heart isn't right.'

Would it be right to stay?

Or would she regret it later?

The questions seemed to fill her mind to the exclusion of everything else and she shook her head. 'I don't know what I want, Matt. Part of me wants to stay but the other part is afraid of what it could mean.'

'Then only you can make the choice, sweetheart. It's your decision and I would never try to persuade you. You have to be sure it's what you want as well.'

He let her go and her heart ached when she saw the sadness in his eyes. 'Let's go and find that oxygen, shall we? You can make up your mind what you intend to do after you've delivered it.'

'And what if I...I decide not to come back?' she whispered, hating herself for hurting him like this. Matt had done everything he could to reassure her and it wasn't his fault that she had these doubts, yet he was paying a high price for them.

'Then I'll understand.'

He smiled at her and her eyes welled with tears when

she saw the tenderness on his face. Even though he was hurt, he still put her first. She turned away because it wasn't fair to let him see that she was upset when it would only upset him more. They went down to the surgery and found the oxygen tank. Catherine added a few more bits and bobs she thought Ann might need then Matt insisted on carrying everything outside and stowing it in the boot of her car.

He closed the boot lid then handed her back the keys. 'Drive carefully, won't you?'

'I will.' Catherine slid behind the wheel and started the engine. She wound down the window, feeling her heart fill with a wealth of emotions at she looked at him standing beside the car.

Was this love? she wondered suddenly. Was this how it felt, this stomach-churning tension, this feeling of anticipation and tenderness all rolled into one? She'd never allowed herself to think about falling in love before so had no way of judging. All she knew was that when she looked at Matt she felt things for him that she had never felt before.

'No pressure, Catherine.' He bent and kissed her gently on the lips and she clung to him, needing his strength to help her reach a decision. It was such a huge step and she was so afraid of making a mistake.

He drew back and there was a shimmer of tears in his eyes as he brushed his knuckles over her mouth in a heartbreakingly gentle caress. 'Take care, sweetheart.'

'And you.'

She left the surgery and drove the short distance to David's house, grateful that the traffic was light at that time of the night. Her thoughts were in complete turmoil so that it was an effort to concentrate as she made her way along the city streets. Ann must have heard her car coming up the drive because she had the front door open by the time Catherine drew up.

Catherine briefly explained that she had offered to deliver the oxygen to save Matt a journey and between them they carried everything inside. Evidently, David was neither better nor worse so she didn't linger once Ann had assured her there was nothing she could do to help.

She drove back down the drive and stopped when she reached the main road. If she turned right then she could be home in ten minutes. She could go into her flat, shut the door and carry on exactly the way she'd planned on doing. However, if she turned left then she would be heading back to the surgery and Matt, to a future that was filled with uncertainties.

What should she do? Should she follow her head or her heart? Matt had said it was her decision, but whatever she decided would affect the rest of her life.

She took a deep breath and flipped on the indicator.

'So if you would take the antenatal clinic this afternoon, that would be a real help. I don't want to disappoint Hannah by not watching her perform at her carol concert, but are you sure you don't mind covering for me, Catherine?'

'Of course I don't mind. I'm happy to do it. Anyway, it's all part of my job, isn't it?'

It was Friday morning, one full week since Matt had asked her to go back to his house, and even now Catherine wasn't sure if she had made the right decision by going home. She might have safeguarded her future plans but there was no denying that the cost had been extremely high.

'Maybe so, but I certainly don't want you to feel that you have to agree out of a sense of duty.'

'I'm not!'

She swallowed the rest of her angry retort because she knew that Matt's prickliness stemmed from his desire to be scrupulously fair. He didn't want her to think that he was behaving any differently towards her than he had before last Friday night. He hadn't mentioned it again or given her the opportunity to do so. Their conversation had centred solely on work throughout the week. Catherine guessed that he didn't want to make her feel uncomfortable, but it wasn't easy for either of them to behave as though nothing had happened.

'I'd like to take the clinic as much for my benefit as yours, Matt,' she said more calmly this time. 'It will be valuable experience for me.'

'I see. Then we're both getting something out of this arrangement. Good.'

He turned to leave but all of a sudden she knew they couldn't go on like this. She had to make him understand that her decision not to go back to the house had had nothing to do with her feelings for him. It was her own fear of losing control of her life that had stopped her taking their relationship a step further.

'Can I have a word with you before you go, Matt?'

'Can it wait?' He glanced at his watch. 'I need to get started on the house calls if I'm to be finished in time for the concert.'

'Of course. Another time, then.'

Catherine's lips pursed as he left the room. She had a sneaking suspicion that he'd guessed what she wanted to talk about. Was he so upset that he couldn't bear to listen to her or was he just not interested any more?

The thought that he might no longer care about her hurt so much that it was impossible to put it out of her mind. Fortunately, there were only half a dozen expectant mothers booked into the clinic that day and no real problems. Ann was there to help her, too—taking blood pressures and writing up the notes. However, it was worrying to realise how the situation was affecting her work. It made her wonder if she should start looking for another job. It might be easier for both her and Matt if she left Brookdale Surgery before her contract ran out.

'Penny for them.'

'Sorry?' Catherine jumped when Ann tapped her on the arm.

Ann laughed. 'I don't know what you were thinking about but you were *miles* away. There's nothing wrong, is there, Catherine?'

'Oh, no, of course not,' Catherine said hurriedly. She glanced at the list on her desk and frowned. 'Was that our last patient?'

'Yes, that's it. A nice early finish for once. It will give me time to pop to the shops before evening surgery starts.' Ann gathered up the files. 'David said that he felt like some fish for dinner tonight so I thought I'd try the fishmonger along the road. I usually buy everything from the supermarket but they don't have a very good selection so I thought I'd try to get something a bit different to tempt him.'

'How is he?' Catherine asked, rolling up her stethoscope and popping it into the drawer.

'Much better, I'm glad to say. The antibiotics have worked a treat.'

'Did the oxygen help or didn't you need to use it?'

'I made David use it for a couple of nights and it definitely helped. In fact, he's now admitted that he was having problems breathing at night even before this happened.'

'It's a common problem for people suffering from motor neurone disease,' Catherine explained. 'The respiratory muscles are often affected and it's even more difficult at night when the patient is lying down.'

'Is there anything you can suggest that might help?' Ann asked worriedly.

'The most effective treatment I know of is non-invasive ventilation via a nasal positive pressure ventilator. Because it doesn't require an artificial airway it doesn't cause problems with coughing or swallowing and there are no after-effects during the day which would inhibit speech.'

'It sounds ideal.' Ann grimaced. 'Do you think you

could mention it to David when you next see him, though? He can be a bit touchy if I suggest anything to him and I don't want to upset things when we seem to be making some progress.'

'Does that mean what I hope it does?' Catherine asked, laughing when Ann blushed. 'I'm so pleased that you managed to talk some sense into him at last. How did you do it?'

'I didn't. I think it was seeing how upset I was when he was so ill that finally convinced him he was making a mistake by cutting me out of his life.' Ann shrugged. 'We had a long talk and I told him what I told you—that I wanted to spend whatever time we have together. It was really easy after that, but I have to be careful because he doesn't like me playing nurse all the time. That's why I'd appreciate it if you explained about that oxygen therapy.'

'Of course I will. Then, if David agrees to try it, we can get things organised.' Catherine smiled. 'I've seen it used and it works extremely well.'

She tidied up after Ann left then fetched her coat. There was quite a good selection of shops close to the surgery so she'd decided to make a start on her Christmas shopping. Normally she would have had it all done by this time but she hadn't bought a thing that year apart from the cards she'd purchased at the school fair. Max and Patricia had invited her for supper on Christmas Eve so she would have to get them a present, plus she wanted to get something for the two receptionists.

She made her purchases, selecting an expensive Italian glass vase for her friends and pretty silk scarves for Margaret and Sharon. She couldn't help thinking how pitiful her two small bags looked compared to what most people were carrying. With Christmas just a week away everyone was loaded down with carrier bags full of goodies but, then, they were probably spending Christmas with their families.

The thought was rather depressing even though the idea

of spending Christmas on her own had never worried her before. She couldn't seem to shake off the feeling as she made her way back to the surgery. Matt was just turning into the drive and she quickened her pace, not wanting to have to speak to him in case he sensed something was wrong. She intended to keep their dealings on a strictly professional footing until they had either resolved their difficulties or she had decided if she should leave. However, she hadn't allowed for the fact that Hannah would spot her.

'Catherine! Catherine, wait!'

Catherine reluctantly stopped, unable to find it in her heart to ignore the little girl. She summoned a smile as Hannah came racing over to her. 'Hello. How did your carol concert go?'

'It was lovely, wasn't it, Daddy?'

'It was.'

Matt had followed her and Catherine felt her heart bump painfully when she turned and saw him standing there. He looked so big and solid that she had the craziest urge to throw herself into his arms. All of a sudden she found herself wishing that she had come back the other night. Then she wouldn't be spending Christmas on her own because she'd be spending it with Matt and his family.

'That's good.' Her voice wobbled despite her resolve to behave with the utmost professionalism around him. The thought of what she had lost that night was just too difficult to deal with. Maybe she *had* safeguarded her plans for the future but she couldn't help wondering if the cost had been far too high.

She quickly excused herself and went to hurry inside before Matt noticed she was upset, but he put a detaining hand on her arm.

'Are you all right, Catherine?'

'I'm fine. Why shouldn't I be?'

'You tell me.' His brows drew together as he subjected her to a searching look that brought the colour rushing to her face. 'You look upset so there's no point trying to pretend that everything is all right because I don't believe you.'

'You're imagining it,' she denied, far too quickly. She bit her lip when she saw the scepticism on his face. Matt obviously didn't believe her and all of a sudden she found herself wondering what she was doing. Why on earth was she lying to him when what she really wanted to do was tell him the truth—that she wished she'd come back and spent the night with him, and that if he asked her again she wouldn't make the same mistake a second time. She didn't want to be on her own this Christmas. She wanted to spend it with him, this Christmas and all the other Christmases to come.

The sheer enormity of that thought stole her breath and she gasped. Was she in love with Matt? Did that explain why she wanted to be with him and why she so regretted turning him down?

She simply didn't know and the fact that she couldn't answer such an important question made her tremble with fear. It was as though her whole life had suddenly run out of her control and was spinning towards mayhem and madness, and she didn't know how to deal with it any more.

'I'll have to go. I need to…to get ready for surgery.'

Catherine's lips felt stiff with shock, her body trembling with tension, and she saw Matt look at her in alarm. She knew she had to get away before he started to question her because she needed to deal with what was happening herself before she tried to explain it to anyone else. If Matt told her that she mustn't worry and that he would take care of everything then she would let him. She would turn her back on all her high ideals about independence without a thought or any care for what she might be doing. The realisation terrified her.

She shrugged off his hand and hurried inside, ignoring him when he called her name. Margaret had returned to work after her bout of flu and she looked up when

Catherine passed the office and said something to her but Catherine shook her head. Whatever the problem was, it would have to wait for a while, maybe even for ever because it might take the rest of her life to get herself back on track after what had happened.

A wave of hysteria gripped her as she went into her room. She had always believed herself to be a person who could cope in a time of crisis but just look at her now. She was a gibbering wreck because she'd suddenly realised that she might have fallen in love with the one person in the world who could turn her life upside down. It would be interesting to see how she dealt with this situation!

'Please, tell me what's wrong, Catherine. I can't bear to see you looking so unhappy.'

She hadn't heard Matt following her into the room and swung round. 'Go away!'

'I'm not going anywhere until you tell me why you're upset.'

He closed the door then walked over to the desk and pressed the button on the intercom. 'Margaret, I'm with Dr Lewis in her office and we are not to be interrupted under any circumstances.'

'You can't do that!' she exclaimed as he cut the connection.

'I just have,' he replied in the sort of no-nonsense tone he might have used when speaking to Hannah. Did he think that she was on a par with a six-year-old child, perhaps, and needed the same kind of firm handling?

Her hysteria bubbled up and she laughed out loud. His mouth tightened as he took a couple of rapid steps that brought him to within touching distance of her.

'Stop it, Catherine. Stop it now.'

He took her gently in his arms, cradling her against him as her laughter suddenly turned to sobs. Catherine clung to him as all her fear rose to the surface, all the pain she had lived with for far too many years. Matt didn't say a word. He just let her cry it all out, his arms steady and comforting around her, his heart beating reassuringly under her cheek. And after a little while her sobs subsided first to sniffles and then to hiccups.

'Better?' His tone was tender, nearly as tender as his expression as he set her from him and looked at her tear-streaked face.

'Yes. I think so...' She tailed off when she felt another wave of tears gather in her eyes. It had been years since she had cried and never like this, as though every tear had been stored up for years and had suddenly found a release.

'Better, but still not right, eh?' He wiped the tears from her cheeks with the pads of his thumbs and her heart contracted on a spasm of pain because nobody had ever behaved so caringly towards her before.

'I'll be OK in a minute,' she murmured, a funny kind of tingling awareness making her stomach churn. Her body seemed to be throbbing in places she hadn't been conscious of before. Her stomach muscles felt as though they'd gone into spasm and there was a heavy feeling between her thighs, a throbbing ache that made her shift uncomfortably as she tried to ease it.

Her head reeled because desire had only ever existed for her before within the pages of a textbook. She'd read about the physical symptoms and understood the mechanics of what was happening but had never experienced them for herself before. If she was honest, she had doubted if the textbooks had been right but now she knew they had been, now when Matt held her like this.

Her eyes were misty with shock when she looked up at him. 'I don't know what's happening to me any more. Everything's such a muddle.'

'I know.' He took her back into his arms and held her tightly as he dropped a feather-light kiss on her lips. 'It's like that for me, too. My head whirls, my body aches and it's all because of you and the effect you have on me, my love.'

'*My love*,' she repeated, wonderingly.

'Yes. My...love...' He interspersed the words with kisses as soft as down, as sweet as honey, and she let out her breath on a tiny sigh. He drew back to look at her and his eyes were very serious all of a sudden. 'We have to do something about this, Catherine. We can't go on this way, can we? We have to accept what's happening and make a decision about what we both want.'

'Do we?' She could hear the panic in her voice, feel her heart beating in short jerky bursts because making a decision like that seemed far too difficult.

'Yes, we do.' He kissed her again just as gently but with aching tenderness, and her panic was overtaken by another emotion. When he set her away from him she would have clung to him if he hadn't taken hold of her hands and held them in his.

'We need to talk this all through but this is neither the time nor the place. Surgery is about to start and we don't want to rush into making a decision we might come to regret. That's why I want you to go home, Catherine.'

'Home? But I can't do that when we have patients arriving to be seen!' she protested.

'Yes, you can. I'll see all the patients tonight. We're not that busy for a change so I'll fit them in somehow. But you're really not in the right frame of mind to deal with other people's problems tonight, are you?'

'No,' she admitted slowly. 'I'm not, but are you sure you can manage, Matt?'

'Quite sure. You go home and I'll come round to your flat after surgery finishes.' He steered her towards the door but she hung back.

'But what about the children? Who'll mind them?'

'I'll work something out so don't worry about it.' He stopped and dropped a kiss on the tip of her nose then opened the door. 'Everything will be fine, Catherine. I promise you. Now, off you go.'

She reached up and kissed him quickly on the lips. 'I hope so, Matt. I really do.'

Neither of them said anything else as they made their way along the corridor. Margaret was obviously agog to know what was going on but Matt simply told her that Catherine was going home and he would be seeing all the patients that evening. Catherine left the surgery and got into her car. Maybe she should have felt guilty about leaving work so early but she knew Matt had been right to send her home. She really couldn't concentrate on other people's problems when she had to resolve her own.

Her hands gripped the steering-wheel so hard that they ached because there was no guarantee that she and Matt would be able to work this out to both their satisfaction. She knew that Matt might want things from her that she couldn't give him. Just because she thought she loved him, it didn't mean the way was clear for them to find ever-lasting happiness. She couldn't just ignore her fears when they had affected the whole of her life.

She bit her lip as panic rose inside her again. Could loving Matt really be enough to compensate for having to give up all her dreams? Maybe—if their feelings for each other lasted and there was no guarantee they would. If she decided to follow her heart then it would be a massive leap of faith, but did she have the courage to make it? Could she really imagine letting herself rely on anyone that completely?

Her heart raced because she couldn't answer either question. She would just have to wait and see.

CHAPTER ELEVEN

CATHERINE decided to call at the delicatessen on her way home. She wasn't sure what time Matt planned on getting to her flat but she doubted if he would stop to have something to eat beforehand. She bought a cooked chicken, a bag of ready-prepared salad—complete with a small sachet of dressing—a loaf of sun-dried tomato bread and then added an expensive bottle of white wine as an afterthought. Matt might not be able to drink it if he was driving, of course, but he would enjoy a glass if he stayed the night.

Her heart almost leapt right out of her chest at that thought. She was all fingers and thumbs as she paid for the shopping and packed it into a carrier bag. She got back into her car and drove home, trying to calm herself down, but it was impossible. Would Matt want to stay the night with her? Would she let him?

She groaned. Why couldn't she make a decision any more? She'd spent the whole of her adult life making choices—what career to choose, where to go to university, where to live—and not once had she experienced the kind of difficulty she seemed to be encountering of late. It just seemed to prove how dangerous it would be to get any more deeply involved than she already was. She'd been content with her life before she'd met Matt and now she had no idea how she felt about anything any longer!

By the time the doorbell rang at a little after seven, Catherine had worked herself up into such a state that she felt physically sick. She ran a smoothing hand over her hair then made herself take a deep breath before she opened the door. Matt gave her a crooked smile.

'Hi! How are you?'

'Fine,' she began, then heaved a sigh. 'A mass of nerves if you want the truthful answer.'

'Me, too.' He stepped inside the hall and gathered her into his arms, pressing his cold cheek to hers as he hugged her close. 'I feel like a kid on his first date—only worse, if you know what I mean. My stomach is churning and my pulse is going crazy. I feel so bad, in fact, that I could very easily pass out, and the idea terrifies the life out of me.'

He drew back and looked at her, his eyes glinting with wry self-mockery. 'I mean, what woman in her right mind would be won over by a guy who collapses at her feet because he's such a wimp he can't handle the pressure?'

Catherine laughed softly and felt her own tension ease a little. 'I've no idea. Most women want a knight in shining armour who'll come charging along to rescue them from the dragon, but it doesn't sound as though you're up for that.'

'No way! I couldn't even get on the wretched horse with my knees knocking like this, let alone stay on it long enough to slay any dragons.' He kissed her softly. 'Want me to leave now so you can phone for a real hero to come and do his stuff?'

'Hmm, I'm not sure it's worth it at this time of the night.' She pursed her lips, loving the small groan he gave as his eyes homed in on her mouth. 'Most heroes are probably busy doing what heroes have to do by now so I may as well stick with you. Anyway, you'll have to stay because I've made supper now and it would be a shame to waste it.'

'You are too kind to a humble knight, my lady.' He swept her a mocking bow then straightened and shrugged off his coat. He dropped it over the hall chair then looked at her. 'Right, I'm all ready for action so what can I do to help? Margaret has very kindly offered to sit with the children so I don't have to worry about rushing back home.'

'In that case, you can open the wine,' she told him,

leading the way to the dining room. She'd laid the pale
beech table with glasses and silverware, and had even
folded the napkins into a complicated pleat. She saw him
pause in the doorway.

'This *is* nice,' he exclaimed appreciatively, taking stock
of the room. 'I love the way you've kept everything so
free from clutter.'

'Do you really like it?' she asked in surprise, glancing
round at the sleek, modern fitments and ivory-white walls.
'It's very different to your house.'

'Which is why I like it so much.' He took the bottle of
wine from her and set to work with the corkscrew. 'Some
days I get the urge to throw out all the clutter and start
again. The trouble is that then I think about how much
time and effort it's going to take to redecorate the place
and go positively weak at the thought.'

Matt grimaced as he removed the cork from the bottle.
'Not much of a catch, am I? I can't slay dragons and I get
cold feet when I think about decorating. I may as well
throw in the towel now.'

'Rubbish! Don't you dare put yourself down. You are a
superb doctor, a wonderful father and your house is exactly
what a family home should be. It's warm and cosy and
safe. No child could ask for a better place to live.'

'Maybe not, but how about you, Catherine? How would
you feel about living there?' He unwound the cork from
the corkscrew and placed it carefully on the table. 'Would
it drive you mad to have to live with all that clutter when
you're used to surroundings like these?'

Catherine bit her lip because she knew Matt's decor
wasn't the real issue. What he was really asking her was
could she imagine being a part of his life with all that it
entailed? Matt came as part of a package and it would be
a massive step to swop her single lifestyle for his.

'Let's leave the difficult questions until later, shall we?'
he suggested, smoothly changing the subject. He poured

wine into the glasses and smiled at her. 'I don't know about you but I always function better on a full stomach.'

'I'll serve supper, then,' she said, relieved to be let off the hook. She went into the kitchen and fetched the plates and the salad. She'd put the bread in the oven to warm so she went back for that then sat down.

Matt cut into his chicken with obvious relish. 'This is good. I hope you didn't go to a lot of trouble, getting it all ready?'

'If you call stopping off at the delicatessen to buy everything as going to a lot of trouble then, yes, I did.' She grinned as she helped herself to salad and passed him the bowl.

He chuckled. 'I like your style! If Mum wasn't around to help out, I'd probably end up doing the same thing.'

'From what I've seen, you're pretty handy in the kitchen,' she retorted, breaking off a piece of the bread and buttering it. 'You're definitely better at using that wretched stove than I am!'

'Oh, there's a knack to it. You'll soon get used to it,' he replied airily.

Catherine didn't say anything but her heart was bumping against her ribs because he seemed to have taken it for granted that she would be cooking in his house at some point in the future. Would she? Could she really see herself in his kitchen, making them all a meal?

Her head whirled as she tried to picture it but the image just wouldn't gel. She popped the bread into her mouth and made herself chew it, wondering if it was an omen. If she couldn't imagine herself as part of his life then maybe it would never happen, and the thought hurt far more than anything had ever hurt before.

'Don't, sweetheart.'

He touched her lightly on the hand and she looked at him with eyes that were shimmering with tears. 'I just can't imagine living in your house, Matt. I can't imagine how it would feel to be part of your life.'

'That's because you don't have anything to base it on.'
He stroked her hand, soothing her. 'I know very little about
your past, Catherine, but I get the impression that you
didn't have a happy home life when you were a child.'

'I didn't. My parents were always arguing so I used to
keep out of their way as much as I could. Then when they
got divorced, my mother was too busy working to spend
much time with me.'

'It must have been very difficult for you. Children are
so influenced by what they see when they are growing up.'

She heard the question in his voice and sighed because
there was no point pretending. 'As I was influenced by
what I saw. I watched my parents fighting, saw how my
mother struggled after they were divorced, listened to her
telling me time after time that the biggest mistake she'd
made was falling in love. It had a huge effect on me. She
used to warn me repeatedly that I must never let myself
rely on anyone because then I could never be let down.'

'Hell!'

His voice grated with pain and she smiled sadly. 'I know
why I'm the way I am, Matt. I make my choices based on
my own experiences and that's why I'm not sure I can
ever be the person you want me to be.'

'That's crazy! Oh, not that you can't be who I want you
to be but that you should imagine I want you to be anyone
except yourself! It's you I love, Catherine. *You*, not some
other woman who doesn't have your history. What happened in your past was what made you the person you are
today, and I don't want you to change.'

'You love me?' she echoed, her mind and her heart
clinging to those words as though they were a lifeline.

'Yes.' He stood up then drew her to her feet as well. 'I
love you. I know it's jumping the gun to tell you that, but
I'm not going to lie to you about how I feel. I'm not even
going to promise you that I'll play fair because I won't.'

He brushed her mouth with a kiss, his lips teasing hers
to part then pulling back the moment they did so that she

was left feeling hungry and frustrated. His eyes gleamed as he looked at her, filled with warmth and something else, something so new and magical that she recognised it immediately as love.

'I am going to do everything in my power to convince you that you belong with me and the girls, that we can be happy and fulfilled together. Maybe it's wrong of me to go about it this way but I'm too desperate to care about the niceties of this situation. I want you, Catherine. I need you. I love you.'

'Matt, I...' She stopped and swallowed because there weren't enough words in the whole English language to describe how she felt at that moment. She was both elated and terrified, filled with joy and awash with fear. Matt was offering her so much but she would have to give up such a lot in exchange and she wasn't sure she could do it.

'I think it's time for the real hard sell,' he murmured.

'Hard sell?'

'Mmm.' He pulled her to him and held her so that she could feel his body throbbing with need. Catherine shivered when she felt an answering pulsing start low in the pit of her stomach then slowly start to spiral up through her whole body. When Matt bent to kiss her she met him halfway, going on tiptoe so that their mouths met with a jolt that sent awareness racing through her like lightning.

Catherine groaned as her mouth clung to his. She could taste the wine on his lips and it just seemed to make the kiss all the more potent. She was trembling when he raised his head, her knees so weak that she would have fallen over if Matt hadn't kept tight hold of her.

'I want to make love to you, Catherine. I want to hold you in my arms and watch your face fill with passion as we love one another, but if it isn't what you want then tell me so.' He kissed her again, his body pulsing against hers, his heart racing almost out of control.

'I...want it, too,' she admitted in a rush. Stepping back, she held out her hand, feeling herself trembling when he took it. He raised it to his lips and kissed each of her fingers in turn then pressed a meltingly tender kiss to her palm.

'It will be all right, my love. You'll see.'

She wished she had his confidence but now wasn't the time to worry about it when her body was clamouring about its needs. She led him to her bedroom, pausing only long enough to turn on the bedside lamp before stepping back into his arms with an eagerness she didn't attempt to disguise.

This time their kiss was so raw and sensual that she cried out and heard Matt mutter something as he quickly began to strip off her clothes. Her skirt landed on the floor and she stepped out of it and kicked it aside then shrugged off her blouse. All she had on now were a lacy bra with matching panties and tights and she saw Matt's jaw clench as he looked at her standing there in the lamplight.

'You're so beautiful,' he gritted out. 'So beautiful that I'm almost scared to touch you.'

'Don't be.' She took his hand and placed it over her racing heart so that he could feel the heavy thunder beating beneath his palm. 'I need you to touch me, Matt.'

A spasm of raw desire crossed his face as he bent and swept her into his arms. He laid her on the bed and she shivered when she felt the chill of the cool cotton sheets against her heated flesh. He quickly undressed then knelt beside her, his eyes holding hers fast as he stroked her skin, starting at her jaw and working his way down until she was twisting and turning in mindless agony at having him tease her that way.

'Please,' she murmured, her eyes half-closed as she felt his fingers sliding under the strap of her bra and start to peel it down her arm. Tension gripped her when she felt the whisper of his breath warm against her naked breast and she stiffened, then cried out when his tongue began to caress her nipple.

'Is this what you want, my love?' he asked, the words tingling against her sensitive flesh.

'Yes!' She took his head between her hands and pulled him down to her again, her whole body jerking when she felt his mouth cover her nipple again and gently suckle it.

He turned his attention to her other breast, lavishing it with just as much attention until it felt as though she was going to explode if she didn't find a release soon. When he stripped off her tights and pants, Catherine helped him, her hands clumsy and urgent as she rid herself of the garments which were preventing her from finding the relief she craved.

Matt moved over her, taking his weight on his elbows as he stared into her face. 'I love you, Catherine. Remember that.'

They were the last words she heard before their bodies joined together. Catherine tensed when she felt a tearing pain rip through her but it lasted only for a second and was instantly forgotten when she felt him thrust inside her. She heard Matt's gasp of shock as he must have realised that she hadn't had sex with anyone before, but she wanted him too much to let him stop.

Her hands gripped his buttocks, urging him on, wanting him to give them both the completion they needed. And he did. As the world erupted into a shower of stars and light she knew that nothing she achieved could be better than this joy she'd found in Matt's arms tonight.

It was almost midnight when Catherine awoke. Matt had made love to her again after that first time—slowly and with great tenderness—and she'd been so worn out and sated by the experience that she'd fallen instantly asleep. Now she sat up and looked at him in dismay.

'I had no idea it was so late! Why didn't you wake me? You need to get home for the children.'

'Don't worry. I phoned Margaret while you were asleep and explained that I'd been held up.' He drew her into his arms and kissed her. 'She told me not to worry what time I got back. I got the feeling that she'd put two and two together and knew where I was.'

Catherine grimaced. 'It won't cause problems, will it?'

'Why should it? We're both adults, Catherine, and it's up to us what we do.'

'But if it got back to the children...'

'It won't. They won't find out unless we want them to.'

She heard the question in his voice and sighed. 'I don't know what to say, Matt.'

'I know, and I understand. This has all happened so fast that it's little wonder you find it difficult to think straight.' He looked at her and his gaze was searching all of a sudden. 'I'm finding it very difficult to believe that you hadn't slept with anyone before, Catherine. It can't have been because of a lack of offers.'

'It just didn't happen,' she admitted, her face heating because she knew how strange it must seem to him. How many women of her age were still virgins in this day and age? Not that she was a virgin any longer, she amended, and blushed even more.

'Because you hadn't met the right person?'

She was overcome by tenderness when she realised that he needed reassuring now. 'No. I never met anyone I wanted to sleep with until I met you, Matt. I always ruled out that it would happen because it seemed...well, safer to steer clear of that kind of involvement.'

'I'm glad. It means that you believe I'm special and that's something to hold onto.' He smiled at her. 'I'm not foolish enough to imagine that everything is all sorted out. You need time to get used to the idea of loving someone, don't you, Catherine?'

'Yes.'

Her heart spasmed with sudden fear because she couldn't help worrying if that was all it entailed. Would her doubts disappear once she got used to the idea of being part of a couple—no, part of a *family*?

She wanted to squash such thoughts out of existence but she couldn't rid herself of them even now. They were too deeply ingrained to be put aside even after what had happened. Maybe Matt sensed her dilemma because he gave her a hug then tossed back the quilt.

'Is it OK if I have a shower? I don't want to take advantage of Margaret's kindness so I'd better get myself home.'

'Of course. There's fresh towels in the basket so help yourself.'

Catherine waited until he'd gone into the bathroom before she got up. She slid her arms into her towelling robe and fastened the belt around her waist. She would have a shower after Matt had left but her hair needed combing if nothing else. It was a mess, half of it hanging down and the rest still pinned into its customary knot.

She sat down at the dressing-table and quickly pulled out the rest of the pins then brushed it smooth. She heard the shower stop and a second later Matt appeared with one of her bath towels wrapped around his waist. His body was hard and lean and she felt her senses stir all over again as she watched him through the mirror. Maybe this had been her first taste of passion but already she was addicted and wanted more.

'If you look at me like that then I'll never get home this side of New Year,' he growled, meeting her eyes in the mirror.

'Sorry.' She looked away, picking up the brush to run it through the long, nut-brown strands of her hair again while passion pulsed and throbbed inside her.

'Don't be sorry. I'd hate it if you didn't feel anything, Catherine.'

He was suddenly standing right behind her so she could feel the steamy heat of his body all down her spine. Catherine bit her lip as she looked up in time to see him bend towards her. The hunger on his face made a mockery of what had happened earlier, as though their love-making had simply whetted his appetite rather than satisfied it.

She closed her eyes when she felt his hands slide inside the collar of her robe, her breath coming in tiny spurts when she felt his fingers caressing her nipples. Tipping back her head, she let it rest against him, almost mindless with pleasure as he caressed her breasts then let his fingers glide down her body to the nest of dark curls between her thighs.

When he pulled her up off the stool and turned her into his arms, she didn't protest because it was what she wanted, too. They made love right there, her buttocks pressed against the hard wood of the dressing-table, her hands gripping his shoulders to stop herself falling over. There was something raw and elemental about their love-making this time, but it was still so wonderfully tender that there were tears in her eyes when it was over. No matter how great his passion, how demanding his hunger, Matt never lost sight of her as a person and it touched her deeply to know how much he cared for her.

'I'll have to go.' He kissed her softly on the mouth then moved away to pick up his clothes. It took only a few minutes for him to get dressed and by that time Catherine had belted her robe and once again smoothed her hair. He took hold of her hand and led her along the hall, stopping by the front door.

'This has been the most wonderful night of my life but I know it hasn't solved all your problems, Catherine. You still have doubts, don't you?'

'Yes. I'm sorry...'

'Don't be sorry. It isn't your fault.' He kissed her again. 'You need more time to put everything into perspective before you decide what you want to do. That's why I want you to spend Christmas with me and the girls. It will give you an idea what you could be letting yourself in for if you do decide that we have a future together.'

'Do you think it's a good idea?' she said worriedly.

'What will Hannah and Becky think if I spend Christmas with you?'

'That at least they're not going to have to put up with just having me to play all those boring games with!' He grinned. 'How are you at Snakes and Ladders and Monopoly?'

'Hopeless! I can't remember when I last played any board games,' she admitted, smiling back.

'Excellent! That means I might have a chance of winning this year.'

'Ah, I see. So there's method in your madness? You want me to spend Christmas with you so you can crow when you win and I lose?'

'Something like that,' he agreed, chuckling. 'So does that mean you'll come for dinner on Christmas Day?'

'Yes, I think it does. On one condition, though.'

'And that is?'

'That I don't have to go anywhere near that wretched oven of yours!'

Matt laughed. 'You won't. Promise.' He kissed her again and hugged her then reluctantly let her go. 'I'd better go. I'll see you on Monday....unless you fancy coming shopping with me tomorrow? I've still got to buy the children's presents and I could really do with some feminine input. So will you? Pretty please with jam on it?'

'All right, then.' She rolled her eyes. 'I hate to see a grown man beg so I suppose I'll have to. What time are you going?'

'Around two if that's OK with you. The girls are going to a birthday party so I can drop them off and come round to collect you. We could try one of those shopping centres on the outskirts of town. We should be able to find a parking place there.'

'I wouldn't bank on it. With only a week to go until Christmas it will be madly busy.'

'Oh, we'll be fine. You'll see. I'll see you tomorrow,

Catherine.' He opened the door then stole a last kiss. 'Sweet dreams, my love.'

'You, too.'

Catherine waited until he'd disappeared into the lift before she closed the door. She went inside and looked around, shivering a little because the central heating had switched itself off and the flat was growing chilly. She turned off the living-room lights then went to have a shower. The bathroom was full of steam and Matt had draped the towel he'd used over the radiator.

She picked it up and buried her face in the damp fabric. It smelled ever so slightly of Matt and her heart tumbled about inside her as she inhaled his scent and remembered what had happened that night. Making love with Matt had been a turning point and she knew that she didn't regret what had happened and never would so why did she feel so afraid all of a sudden? Because now that he'd left she had nobody to reassure her?

Her heart raced but this time its rhythm had nothing to do with her feelings for him and everything to do with herself. How quickly she had come to rely on him but what if he let her down? How would she cope then? Surely it would be better if she never put herself in the position of having her heart broken?

She hung the towel back on the rail and there was a cold feeling of dread inside her which felt worse after the heat of passion. She didn't want to have these doubts but she couldn't help it. Her fears were so deeply ingrained and so much a part of her that she might never be able to overcome them. Loving Matt might not be enough.

CHAPTER TWELVE

'THIS really wasn't the best idea I've ever had!'

Catherine laughed when she heard the disgust in Matt's voice. He had picked her up at two o'clock on Saturday afternoon and driven them to a shopping centre on the outskirts of the city. The traffic had been horrendous so it had taken them twice as long as they'd expected to get there. Then when they'd arrived they had discovered the car park was full. They were currently stuck in a long line of cars, all waiting to find a parking space.

'I did warn you,' she murmured, earning herself a speaking look.

'You did so there's no need to crow.' He put his head in his hands and groaned. 'How can a mere male be expected to deal with this? You women must have a lot more stamina than we do to cope with the run-up to Christmas.'

'Oh, I think it's widely accepted now that we are the superior sex,' she quipped, pleased that Matt seemed determined to keep the mood light.

She had spent the night and most of the morning worrying about the problems surrounding their relationship. She'd got herself into such a state at one point that she'd even considered phoning Matt to cancel their shopping trip. However, she'd known in her heart that she would never be able to resolve the situation if she kept avoiding the issue. In the event, she needn't have worried because Matt had set the tone from the outset, keeping the conversation to impersonal topics rather than what was probably uppermost on both their minds. She felt a sudden rush of affection at his thoughtfulness and leant over to kiss him on the cheek.

'I don't know what I've done to deserve that but thank you very much.' He grinned at her and Catherine felt her heart lift when she saw the warmth on his face. Despite her reservations, she couldn't pretend that it didn't feel wonderful to know how much she meant to him.

'I'll even forgive you for that cheap shot about women being the superior sex. I can't say fairer than that, can I?'

'You certainly can't.' She grimaced as the car in front crawled another few yards closer to the parking lot. 'At this rate it will be time to go home before we get any shopping done!'

'I know. It was a lousy idea to come here.' He glanced at the dashboard clock and sighed. 'We're not going to have much time to do the shopping at this rate. I have to collect the girls from their party at half past six.'

'Why don't we give it up as a bad job and try the shops near the surgery? There's a book shop and a toy shop so you should be able to find something there for Hannah. There's also a store that sells some rather nice clothes for teenagers which Becky might like.'

'That sounds like a much better idea to me than sitting here in this queue.'

Matt quickly pulled out of the queue. He turned the car around and headed back the way they'd come, letting out a heartfelt sigh once they had left the tailback behind. 'That's better! I could feel my stress levels creeping up to overload while we were sitting there.'

'You men just aren't programmed for that kind of situation. Your shopping gene is missing.'

'It is, and I for one don't regret it!' He laughed as he captured her hand. Catherine shivered when he delicately kissed her fingertips. 'Have I told you how much I love you, Dr Lewis?'

'You did mention it,' she said, struggling to maintain her smile. She knew how hard it must be for him but she found it difficult to cope when he was so open about his feelings.

Matt must have realised how she felt because he quickly released her. 'Sorry. I didn't mean to spoil things. I know you don't feel the same way I do.'

'I don't know how I feel,' she corrected gently, hating to hear him sounding so deflated. 'This is all very new to me, Matt, and I find it hard to put a name to what I'm feeling. I know how difficult it must be for you to understand, but I don't want to lead you on. I...I could never live with myself if I hurt you.'

'And I couldn't live with myself if I made you unhappy so let's not think about it any more. Let's just enjoy being together and leave it at that for now. There will be time enough for us to decide what we want after Christmas, won't there?'

Catherine didn't reply. She wished she could be as certain as he seemed to be that everything would become clear after Christmas. Matt still seemed to believe that it was simply a case of her getting used to the idea of loving him, but she knew there was more to it than that. She had to find the courage to change her whole way of life and it wasn't going to be easy. Still, maybe he'd been right to tell her not to worry about it. She'd spent hours thinking about the situation and had still not come up with any answers so maybe she should give herself a breathing space.

They drove back to the surgery and parked in the drive. Matt locked the car and held out his hand. 'Come along, then, let's get this show on the road. We have two hours to make sure that Hannah and Becky aren't disappointed when they see what Santa has brought them this year.'

Catherine laughed as she slipped her hand into his. 'Sounds like rather a tall order to me. You don't really think we'll get all the shopping done in a couple of hours, do you?'

'I don't just think it. I know we will!' He swung her round to face him and kissed the tip of her nose. 'Faint heart never got Christmas all wrapped up so jump to it, young lady!'

'Aye, aye, Cap'n,' she replied saucily. She skipped smartly out of the way when he made a grab for her. 'Too slow! You'll need to be a lot quicker than that if you hope to catch me.'

'Will I, indeed?'

He made another lunge for her and Catherine laughed as she turned and fled down the drive. He soon caught up with her, pulling her into his arms and turning her round so that he could dole out a suitable punishment. His face was cold from the winter air but his lips were filled with fire and her laughter disappeared beneath a sudden surge of passion. When he let her go she clung to him for a moment, unable to shake off the feeling of completeness that had filled her, the sense that she could find everything she needed right there in his arms.

Maybe this *was* love after all, she thought wonderingly. And maybe it *could* last for ever. Just because her parents hadn't found lasting happiness together, it didn't mean that she and Matt couldn't achieve it.

Her head spun as they made their way along the road. She had always kept her emotions strictly under control because she'd been afraid of getting carried away. It wasn't easy to let go but she had to try. Maybe she wouldn't be able to give Matt what he wanted from her but at least he would have the consolation of knowing that she had done her best to overcome her fears because of him.

By the time five o'clock arrived they had visited every shop in the road and were loaded with parcels. Catherine groaned when Matt balanced yet another box on top of the pile she was carrying. 'Surely that should be enough by now?'

'It is. I never thought we'd do so well and it's all thanks to you. If you hadn't been with me then I would *never* have thought of buying Becky that sweater or those jeans.

They looked so...well, grown up.' He sighed. 'I still tend to think of her as a little girl and forget that she's turning into a young woman.'

'I do have a slight advantage over you,' she pointed out, stopping on the edge of the kerb while they waited for the lights on the pedestrian crossing to change. There were a lot of people waiting to cross and she moved aside when a young woman with a pushchair and a small child in tow squeezed into the gap beside her. The baby was crying its head off and Catherine had to raise her voice to make herself heard.

'I was a teenage girl in the dim and distant past so I know how important it is to have the latest fashions. I used to spend hours poring over teen magazines when I was in the children's home, choosing all the wonderful trendy things I'd love to wear even though there was very little chance of me ever having them.'

'I hate to think what a rotten childhood you must have had,' he began sadly then suddenly gasped. 'No! Come back!'

Catherine felt her heart leap into her throat when she turned to see who he was shouting to and saw that the little girl who'd been standing beside them had wandered into the road. Everything seemed to be a blur after that. She saw Matt drop his parcels as he darted forward and swept the child into his arms, heard the screech of brakes as the car that had been heading towards the crossing tried to stop. It hit Matt a glancing blow, sending him tumbling onto the tarmac.

The child's mother started screaming but Catherine was too shocked to react. Matt was lying in the road, not moving, and she could only stare at him in horror. It was only when the driver of the car got out and pleaded for help that she finally managed to respond.

Dropping her parcels onto the pavement, she ran into the road and knelt down beside Matt. 'I'm a doctor,' she told the young man. 'Let me see.'

'I couldn't stop. I saw him run out and grab the kid but I just couldn't stop in time!'

He suddenly sank onto the ground but Catherine ignored him as she bent over Matt. The driver didn't appear to be hurt so she could safely leave it to the paramedics to deal with him when they arrived. Someone was bound to have phoned for an ambulance by now so she would concentrate on Matt and the child.

The little girl was screaming but she didn't appear to be badly injured. Matt had taken the brunt of the impact, using his body to shield the child. Catherine quickly checked her over but so far as she could tell the little girl was simply shocked. She beckoned the child's mother over and handed the toddler to her.

'I don't think she's hurt. She's probably more shocked than anything, but she'll need to be examined properly in hospital. Just try to keep her calm, will you?'

'I didn't see her let go of the pram,' the young woman wailed as she cuddled the little girl. 'She's never, *ever* run into the road like that before!'

Catherine didn't say anything. She was more concerned about how badly injured Matt was to waste any time by pointing out that it only needed the child to do it once to result in a tragedy. 'Matt, can you hear me?' she said urgently, her fingers searching for and finding the pulse below his jaw. The rhythm was steady and regular and she breathed a sigh of relief although she would have felt even better if he'd answered her.

She ran her fingers over his skull and grimaced when she felt a lump behind his left ear. He'd obviously hit his head on the tarmac when he'd fallen, which probably explained why he was unconscious. There was no way of telling how serious the injury might be until they got him to hospital so she quickly checked him for fractures. She ran her hands down his arms and legs, checked his hips and tested each of the vertebrae in his spine, but from what she could tell everything was fine. However, when she slid her hand along his left collar-bone, he moaned.

'Matt, can you hear me?' she demanded, her heart thumping as she bent over him. 'Does that hurt?'

'Hurts like hell,' he muttered, and she gave a choked little laugh of sheer relief at his grumpy tone.

'It's your own fault for playing the hero. Now, lie still while we wait for the ambulance to get here.'

'Don't need an ambulance' he grumbled, glowering at her. 'It was just a bit of a bump, that's all.'

'I'll be the judge of that, thank you very much.'

'Has anyone ever told you that you're a bully, Catherine Lewis?'

'Loads of people, and it didn't make a scrap of difference so you may as well shut up and do as you're told.'

One of the shopkeepers arrived then with some blankets so she draped one over him then checked to see how the little girl was faring. She had stopped crying and seemed to be fine now that she had got over her shock. Catherine knew how fortunate the child had been because if Matt hadn't managed to grab her she could have been killed.

She helped the mother wrap the child in a blanket then asked one of the bystanders to fetch the young woman's pram over in the hope that it would calm down the baby. The assistant from the toy shop had collected all their parcels and she came over to tell Catherine that she would take them into the shop for safekeeping.

Catherine thanked her then checked Matt again, taking his pulse and checking his eyes…or at least the one eye that was visible. She still hadn't turned him over and had no intention of doing so until the paramedics got there. Although there didn't appear to be any damage to his spine, she didn't intend to take any chances and would wait until they had the right equipment before she moved him.

'I'm fine,' he complained. 'I'm just a bit bruised and sore but there's no need to fuss. Really!'

'Good. I'm pleased to hear it but you still aren't getting up,' she said firmly. She glanced round when the sound of a siren announced that the ambulance was on its way. 'Here's the ambulance now.'

She told the paramedics what had happened and they insisted on strapping Matt to a spinal board to his disgust and her relief. She climbed into the ambulance and sat down beside him while a paramedic closed the doors. The mother had gone in a second ambulance with the little girl and her baby so they were saved having to listen to the poor mite screaming its head off. A policeman was taking statements from the driver and some of the people who had witnessed the accident. Catherine knew they would need to give statements, too, but they could wait for now. Getting Matt to hospital was her number-one priority.

Matt continued to complain all the way to the hospital but Catherine ignored him. He was going to be examined whether he liked it or not! The paramedics took him straight into Resus while Catherine went to give his details to the admitting clerk. She rattled it all off—his name, age, address and profession. She gave his mother's name as his next of kin then explained that Mrs Fielding was out of the country because it was important that the staff had the correct information to hand in case anything happened.

All of a sudden her legs turned to jelly as the full horror of what had happened hit her. Matt might have been killed and the staff would have needed the information so they could make the necessary arrangements. The thought left her feeling so completely devastated that she couldn't reply when the young man behind the counter asked her to sit down until the doctor was ready to speak to her.

She made it to a chair and sank down. She felt so sick and shaken that she wondered if she was going to faint. She simply couldn't imagine what she would have done if Matt had been killed. The thought of him no longer existing seemed to shake the very foundations of her world. She needed to see him and touch him, smell him and speak to him for there to be any meaning to her life. She didn't give a damn about the wonderful career she had planned for herself. She only cared about Matt and the realisation stunned her. She had done the one thing she had sworn never to do—she had fallen in love. The only question now was did she have the courage to tell him that?

It was almost half an hour before the doctor came to find her. Catherine got up as soon as she saw him leaving Resus and hurried to meet him. 'How is he?'

'Not too bad, considering. He's got a fractured clavicle, but that will soon heal and shouldn't cause any problems. I'm more concerned about the bump on his head and the fact that he lost consciousness so I'm sending him down for a CT scan. Obviously, it will depend on what we find but we'll be keeping him in at least for tonight.'

'Can I see him before he goes for the scan?' she asked quickly.

'I don't see why not,' the doctor replied cheerfully. 'Pop on through to Resus and tell the nurse I said it was OK. The paramedics said you were a doctor so I don't need to give you the usual spiel about not worrying about all the tubes, do I?'

'No,' she replied shakily, because it was rather different being on the receiving end of all the medical expertise. She might understand why Matt needed the equipment but it wouldn't make it any easier to see him like that.

She made her way into the resuscitation room and explained to the nurse that she'd been given permission to see Matt. He was lying on a bed, looking extremely sorry for himself. There were various lines and tubes attached to him but Catherine steadfastly ignored them as she visually checked him over. There was a nasty-looking graze down his left cheek and his left arm was in a sling to support the broken clavicle, but apart from that he looked fine. She was overwhelmed by relief so it was an effort to behave casually as she went to the bed.

'Hi! The doctor said I could pop in and see you. How do you feel?'

'As though I've been trampled by a herd of elephants.' He grimaced. 'How's the little girl? Have you heard anything?'

'Not yet but she seemed to be fine from what I could tell. A bit shaken up and obviously scared but nothing to worry about,' she assured him.

'That's good.' He rested his head against the pillows and sighed. 'I've got to have a CT scan, apparently.'

'So the doctor told me. And they're keeping you in overnight as a precaution.'

'But I can't stay here! What about the girls?' He frowned. 'What time is it? I'm supposed to pick them up from the party at half past six.'

'It's almost six now,' Catherine told him, checking her watch. She could tell how agitated he was getting and hurried on. 'Look, just tell me where they are and I'll fetch them.'

'Would you? That would be great but are you sure you don't mind, Catherine?'

'Of course I don't mind!'

He rattled off the address then looked at her in dismay. 'But what's going to happen tonight if they keep me in? Becky and Hannah are too young to be left in the house on their own.'

'They won't be on their own because I'll stay with them, of course.'

'You will?'

'Yes, so stop worrying!' She glanced round when the nurse tapped her on the shoulder and told her that it was time for Matt to go to the radiology unit.

'I'll have to go now. Don't worry about the girls because I'll sort everything out and they'll be fine.'

'I know they will if you're with them,' he said huskily. 'Thank you, Catherine. I really appreciate this.'

'I'm happy to do it.'

She bent and kissed him quickly on the lips then stood up. All of a sudden her heart was drumming inside her but she knew what she had to do. She looked him in the eyes and felt a wave of love wash over her. This man meant the whole world to her and she would do anything in her power to make their relationship work. 'It will be good practice for me, Matt.'

'Good practice? What do you mean?'

She touched him lightly on the cheek. 'I need to get used to being part of your family if we're going to be spending a lot of time together.'

'Catherine!'

She laughed when she heard the shock in his voice. There was no time to say anything else because the porter was waiting to take him down to Radiography. Catherine left the hospital and hailed a taxi so she could collect Becky and Hannah from the party. They were both surprised to see her and upset when she explained about their father's accident.

They were desperate to see him so they got another taxi back to the hospital. Catherine left them in the waiting room while she went to check on Matt and was relieved when she was informed that he had been transferred to the observation ward. The CT scan had shown no signs of any serious injury to his brain so he was being treated for mild concussion and would be monitored overnight.

The ward sister only allowed them to see him for a few minutes but it was long enough to reassure the children. Catherine kept out of the way so he could concentrate on the girls because it was more important that they shouldn't worry. She just had time for a brief word with him before the sister told them it was time to leave, but she could see the love in his eyes when he wished her a husky goodnight and that was more than enough to keep her going.

They went back to Matt's house and phoned for a pizza then spent the evening playing games. Catherine tucked Hannah into bed and kissed her goodnight, smiling when the little girl clung to her.

'Are you going to stay all night, Catherine?'

'I am. So you don't need to worry because I'll be right here if you need me.'

'Good.' Hannah planted a noisy kiss on her cheek. 'I love you, Catherine.'

'I love you, too, poppet,' she whispered, her eyes brimming with tears because it was true. Somewhere along the line Matt's children had found a place in her heart as well and her life would be all the richer because of it.

She went to bed when Becky did, feeling a strange sense of rightness as she went into Matt's room and turned on the bedside lamp. She didn't have any nightclothes with her but she found one of his old T-shirts in a drawer and used that for a nightshirt. The cotton was soft from many washes and she snuggled it around her, pretending that it was his arms wrapped around her.

She slid into the big double bed and pressed her face into the pillows, drinking in his scent. It felt wonderfully and marvellously right to be there in his bed in his house, with his children sleeping just across the landing from her. Maybe she would have to alter her plans for the future but there wasn't any doubt in her mind that it would be worth it.

On that happy thought she fell asleep and was woken the next morning shortly after seven by someone kissing her cheek. She rolled over, half expecting to see Hannah, and gasped when she found Matt sitting on the side of the bed.

'What are you doing here? You're supposed to be in hospital!'

'The registrar agreed to let me leave,' he murmured, bending so he could press his mouth to her bare shoulder where the oversized T-shirt had fallen away.

Catherine shivered when she felt him delicately nibble her skin and felt him smile.

'I think he was glad to see the back of me, to be honest. He was probably fed up with me grumbling about being kept in. He certainly didn't put up much of a fight when I told him I was leaving with or without his permission.'

'You didn't?' She shook her head when he grinned. 'You crazy man. You know very well how important it is to monitor a person after they've lost consciousness!'

'Is that a fact?' His mouth slid from her shoulder to her throat so he could trail kisses up to her jaw. 'But I wanted to be here with you.'

'And I wanted you to be here, too,' she admitted huskily. 'But it would have been very silly to have come home after that bump you had.'

'I know. It's just that I couldn't sleep a wink from thinking about you being here in my bed.' His lips moved a little higher so that he could drop a kiss on the corner of her mouth and she groaned.

He grinned wickedly as he drew back a fraction. 'If you want me to stop then just say the word.'

She glowered at him. 'It would serve you right if I did tell you to stop. You're getting a little above yourself, Dr Fielding.'

'Sorry, but it's your fault, not mine.'

'Oh, and how do you work that out?'

'Simple. You look so adorable in my T-shirt that I can't keep my hands off you.' He glanced at his sling and pulled a face. 'Make that hand—singular, not plural.'

'There's an easy solution to that. I can always take the T-shirt off if it's bothering you.'

She sat up and took hold of the soft cotton fabric and drew it over her head. Her heart began to race when she heard him take a shuddering breath as he looked at her sitting there, her skin all warm and flushed with sleep.

'Is that better?' she asked softly.

'Oh, yes! Much, much better,' he ground out, bending

forward so that he could kiss her. Catherine sank back against the pillows and pulled him to her, taking care not to jolt his injured shoulder. They kissed for a long time, kisses that said more than any amount of words could have done about how they felt. Matt drew back and looked at her and she thought she was going to burst with happiness when she saw the expression in his eyes.

'I love you, Catherine. I think I know how you feel about me but I'd still like to hear you say it.'

'I love you, too, Matt.' It came out as a whisper and she laughed as she repeated it much more loudly. 'I love you! I never thought I'd say that to any man but I mean it with my whole heart.'

'That's all I needed to hear, sweetheart. We can sort the rest out later.'

He pulled her towards him and kissed her with a hunger that immediately had her clinging to him. Catherine helped him undress and then they made love—wild, glorious and uninhibited love that set the seal on their feelings for each other. There wasn't a doubt left in her mind any longer about what she was doing and it felt as though a huge weight had been lifted from her shoulders all of a sudden.

She was free to be herself at last, free to find happiness with this man who would never hurt her but always cherish her. She had to be the luckiest woman alive.

Christmas Eve...

'That's it. The last present wrapped and now all we need to do is fill the girls' stockings.'

Catherine sat back on her heels and looked in satisfaction at the mound of gaily wrapped parcels strewn across the living-room floor. It was almost midnight and she had been wrapping and tying ribbons for almost three hours. Of course, the fact that Matt had kept hindering her attempts to get the job done hadn't helped speed things up, but she hadn't really objected. Why should she object because the man she adored seemed unable to keep his hands off her?

'I certainly couldn't have managed without you, Catherine.' He came and sat beside her on the floor, pulling her to him while he rewarded her with yet another delicious kiss on her mouth.

Catherine shuddered appreciatively, her lips clinging to his as though they never wanted to be free again. The past few days had been the most wonderful of her entire life so that sometimes she found herself wondering if she was dreaming. She and Matt had spent every single minute together after work and she'd been stunned to discover just how easily she had slotted into his life. Now she couldn't imagine being without him and told him so, earning herself another even more tender kiss.

'I love you so much, sweetheart.' He drew back and looked at her. 'I don't know how I've managed all these years without you, in fact.'

'I know what you mean.' She laughed softly. 'Some days I wake up and wonder what I did before I fell in love with you. My life just seems one big nothing.'

'You grew into the beautiful woman I love.'

'So you're happy with me, warts and all?' she teased.

'I'm not so sure about the warts,' he replied, then held up his hand when she threatened him with the roll of Christmas wrapping paper. 'Mercy! Would you really hit an injured man?'

'If he continues to be cheeky then, yes, I would!'

'Uh-oh! I'd better do something to get back into your good books, hadn't I?' He got up and went to the bureau then came back with a rather lumpy-looking parcel. 'It will be hectic tomorrow when the children wake up so I wanted to give you your present tonight,' he explained.

Catherine grinned as she got up and took it from him. 'I take it that you wrapped it all by yourself?'

'One-handed, no less,' he assured her, laughing. 'If

you've ever tried peeling off sticky tape *and* holding the paper together with one arm in a sling, you'll understand why it's not the best-wrapped present in the world!'

'It's lovely, all the more so because you bothered to wrap it,' she assured him, sitting down on the sofa. She quickly peeled off the paper and gasped when she saw what it contained. 'It's the box we bought at the Christmas fair! Oh, it looks gorgeous now all the shells have been replaced. Thank you so much.'

'I'm glad you like it but your real present is inside.'

'It is?'

She opened the lid and frowned when she saw that the box contained the photograph of Matt and the girls which was normally kept on his desk in the surgery. She took it out of the box as Matt came and sat down beside her. He took hold of her hand and held it tightly as he looked into her eyes.

'This is my real present to you, Catherine. I'm offering you myself and the girls, and I can only hope that you will accept the gift.'

'You and the girls,' she repeated, tears filling her eyes as she looked at the picture.

'Yes. I want you to marry me, Catherine. I know it will mean that your life won't work out the way you had planned it, but I swear that I will do everything in my power to make you happy.'

He kissed her gently on the mouth but she could feel his tension and suddenly realised that he wasn't sure what her answer was going to be. A wave of tenderness washed over her as she kissed him back and held him against her heart because there weren't any doubts in her mind even if there were some in his!

'Of course I'll marry you, Matt, if you're sure it's what you and the girls want.'

'It is. Oh, it is!' He hugged her to him then groaned when his injured shoulder protested at his enthusiasm.

'What a time to be incapacitated,' he grumbled, relaxing his grip just a little.

Catherine chuckled as she kissed him on the mouth. 'You will have to be patient. It will be another couple of weeks before your shoulder heals completely.'

'I don't *feel* like being patient,' he retorted, then sighed. 'Sorry! You'll be changing your mind if I carry on being such an old grump. You won't, will you?' he added worriedly.

'No. I'm going to marry you come hell or high water,' she assured him.

'Good.' He suddenly sobered. 'I know you'd set your heart on starting up your own practice, darling, so if you still want to go ahead with it then I want you to know that I shall do everything in my power to help you.'

'Thank you. That means a lot to me but the truth is that it no longer seems quite so important. Maybe I'll see if a certain GP will offer me a job when my contract expires.'

'You mean that?' He smiled in delight when she nodded. 'That would be wonderful!'

'Glenda might not be so keen on the idea,' she pointed out.

'Oh, yes, she will. She'll be absolutely thrilled about it. We desperately need a third partner and it would be perfect if you would consider taking the job, Catherine. I can't believe it. We'll be able to work together and live together!''

'You might get sick of me,' she warned.

'No way. Never in a million years! To misquote those stickers you see in the back of cars, *Love is for life not just for Christmas.*'

He kissed her hungrily, telling her in the most effective way possible that he meant that. Catherine's heart swelled with love as she kissed him back. She had found true love and it would last for ever and she was sure of that. She and Matt would build a wonderful life for themselves and their family.

A sudden smile curled her mouth because next Christmas there might even be an addition to their family.

'What are you smiling about?' Matt murmured.

'I'll tell you later…'

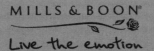

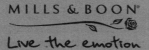

MILLS & BOON®

BETTY NEELS

THE CHRISTMAS COLLECTION

On sale 5th December 2003

*Available at most branches of WH Smith, Tesco, Martins, Borders,
Eason, Sainsbury's and all good paperback bookshops.*

FREE!

4 Books
and a surprise gift!

We would like to take this opportunity to thank you for reading this Mills & Boon® book by offering you the chance to take FOUR more specially selected titles from the Medical Romance™ series absolutely FREE! We're also making this offer to introduce you to the benefits of the Reader Service™—

- ★ FREE home delivery
- ★ FREE gifts and competitions
- ★ FREE monthly Newsletter
- ★ Books available before they're in the shops
- ★ Exclusive Reader Service discount

Accepting these FREE books and gift places you under no obligation to buy; you may cancel at any time, even after receiving your free shipment. Simply complete your details below and return the entire page to the address below. *You don't even need a stamp!*

YES! Please send me 4 free Medical Romance books and a surprise gift. I understand that unless you hear from me, I will receive 6 superb new titles every month for just £2.60 each, postage and packing free. I am under no obligation to purchase any books and may cancel my subscription at any time. The free books and gift will be mine to keep in any case.

M3ZEF

Ms/Mrs/Miss/Mr ....Initials................................
BLOCK CAPITALS PLEASE

Surname..

Address..

....

....Postcode ....

Send this whole page to:
UK: The Reader Service, FREEPOST CN81, Croydon, CR9 3WZ
EIRE: The Reader Service, PO Box 4546, Kilcock, County Kildare (stamp required)